DEATH NEVER CHANGES

MICHAEL McCLENDON

AF472454

All rights reserved. No part of this book may be reproduced in any form or by any electronic or mechanical means including information storage and retrieval systems, without permission in writing from the author or publisher. The only exception is by a reviewer, who may quote short excerpts in a review.

This book is a work of fiction. Names, characters, places, and incidents either are products of the author's imagination or are used fictitiously. Any resemblance to actual persons, living or dead, events, or locales is entirely coincidental.

Text copyright © 2015 by Michael McClendon

Cover Graphics Sarah Hotard

Layaya Press in association with Zing Publishing

www.Layaya.org

Printed in the United States of America

www.MMcClendon.com

This novel is dedicated with love and appreciation to my family.

Thank you for your encouragement, inspiration and support. I could never have done this without you!

Special Thanks

I would like to thank Layaya and Ms. Jo. Without her none of this would have been possible.

I would also like to thank my fifth grade English teacher for helping me find my love of writing.

I would like to thank my sixth grade history teacher Mrs. Lacobe.

Many thanks to my seventh grade English teacher, Ms. Martinez. She was one of the reasons that I wrote the first edition.

I would also like to thank my eighth grade English teacher Mrs. McGar, for editing some of the first pages and encouraging me.

My appreciation goes to Sarah Hotard, a fellow Layaya member and the amazing artist who offered her talents to design this cover of Death Never Changes.

To all the people in my life who inspire and support me, those named and those not named - Thank you. I could not have done this without all of you.

Very special thanks to Mr. B. Flores and Mr. W. Plasse

PROLOGUE

Death. Death is all I see anymore. I always wished for this to happen; I had a plan and everything. I mean you always want to get out of school, right? Sometimes we all want to get out of reality, and sometimes you just want to get out of society as we know it. We all just want to be in a place where no one judges you.

Every high school student hopes for this at some point.

You rarely consider that the dead would have to rise for it to happen.

We all wanted an apocalypse to happen. Being teens sometimes means being short sighted…and not considering that the excitement of a movie plot never really translates well into real life; especially when it means the death of family and friends. After three months of seeing death you'd think I'd have given up on life, just sit and wait for the curtains to close, the white light to shine on me and take my soul away. I have a few people left to live for. I just can't let myself die. I have to be a shining light for my people.

I need to be more than just a survivor; I need to be a leader.

The timing of death, like the ending of a story, gives a changed meaning to what preceded it.

~Mary Catherine Bateson

CHAPTER 1

FELIX

The day it all starts, I am just getting out of my fifth period class. My teacher holds me back after class to yell at me for finishing my class work and reading when I was supposed to be working with my group. My fifth period teacher was Ms. Caldwell – she really disliked me with a passion   After she says go, I rush through the door and find my friends in the ocean-like wave of students rushing to sixth period class. About half way to my next class I spot them standing by the water fountains. I see my best friend, John Greene, and his girlfriend, Emily Monroe, talking to my girlfriend, Trinity Rowe. I make my way towards them. Before I even get to them John turns around and almost yells, "What is up Mane?" Mane is the nickname John and I call each other. I respond, "Nothing, but the sky." We laugh and fist bump. The tardy bell rings and we move as a group to our next class.

We have the next two classes together. After thirty seconds of navigating the angry ocean of students, we make it to our sixth period class. When we reach the doorway, we are met by our favorite teacher, Ms. Martini. She is a twenty-six old ELA teacher with blonde hair who actually knows what she is doing. She greets us and we enter the class room. After we enter, all four of us head to our seats, next to three of our friends – Christian Ore, Billy Price, and Tom Donavan.

When we sit down Ms. Martini walks in. She closes the door and heads to her desk. "Alright class, take out your notebooks and respond to the question on the board."

I start to take out my notebook, but before I can even open it an ear piercing scream erupts from somewhere in the hallway. It destroys the wall of silence outside the classroom. After just about a minute, the unbearable screeching stops.

After it stops we all take our hands off of our ears. The first one to speak is me.

"Martini, it may be a person in distress." The whole class looks at me and even Martini is staring at me with a dumbfounded look. Martini starts to get out of her desk.

"Now, Felix, we can't do anything about it. So what I am going do is call the office." I nod and hope it has nothing to do with the reports of cannibalism that has been all over the news.

She starts for the speaker mounted by the door. When, she gets close enough, she hits the red button that connects the speaker to the office. After, she hits the button; it takes the office thirty seconds to respond.

"Hello, Ms. Martini."

"Hello, my class and I heard a strange scream."

There is a pause before the lady over the intercom responded.

"Well, Ms. Martini, we don't know what you're talking about."

"Well, I know I heard something." When the intercom lady responds we all know something is wrong when there is a moan and a crash. We all look at the intercom like a family listening to the radio after a bomb attack. After thirty seconds, the principal comes over the intercom.

"Students and staff listen to me; this isn't a drill. There is no intruder; there is something even worse." He pauses, and we can hear his breathing go coarse. "Get out of the school while you can. Go. Don't even think about it; leave."

"GET BACK. OH GOD NOT LIKE THIS, I WAS ONLY TWO MONTHS AWAY FROM RETIREMENT!" The intercom goes silent with a scream.

After about thirty seconds, the whole school goes crazy. All I hear outside in the hallway is the sound of terrified children rushing and trampling people to get away from certain death. Even teachers are trampling kids. The whole school turns to hell. Everyone is trying to escape it. The first ones to move in my room are the students I never gave a flying fart about.

My friends and I don't move; neither does Ms. Martini. After the less important students leave, Martini gets the bat that she keeps behind her desk in case of intruders and her phone. I stand up and say to my friends and Martini.

"I'm going to get Malcobe."

She and my friends just look at me dumfounded and Martini is the first one to speak.

"Now Felix, you know she probably left right?" I look at her and start to move towards the door.

I look at her and start to move towards the door, "No she hasn't, she brought Elliot to school today." Elliot is Ms. Malcobe's kid.

"Do you really think that she would leave while the crowds are trampling each other?"

She nods and starts to speak. "You can't just go alone. You have to have people with you to watch your back; and what about the rest of us?" I stay silent for a second after that.

"You have a point there. I can't go alone, that's why John is coming with me, and the rest of you will get in your car and go to my house."

John looks at me. "I am?"

"Yes, John, you are going with me."

Trinity and Emily stand up and say in unison, "How will you two get to your house?"

"Girls, girls, girls, we'll just ride with Malcobe and meet you at the house." They nod and we get our personal stuff from our book bags. The only thing I get out of my bag is my phone.

. . .

John and I exit the school with the rest of the group to ensure they get to Martini's car safely. Luckily, nothing happens. Before Martini, Emily, Trinity, Billy, Christian, and Tom, get in the car, we say our goodbyes, and I hug both girls and even hug the guys in case this crazy plan is the one that kills me.

Everybody gets in the car except for Trinity. She hugs me one more time and whispers into my ear.

"You, better make it back; if you die here, I will kill you."

Before she can say anything I start to talk. "See ya in about an hour or two." She smiles and I kiss her one more time and let go of her.

When she gets in the car, I close the door behind her and walk to the steps of the school with John. We wave to them as they drive out of the school parking lot and into the swarming traffic. The traffic looked like a hurricane was coming.

John and I look up into the soft blue sky, clear of clouds. We feel the tingly sensation of the nice warm sun on our skin. We do this for almost five minutes before we walk back into our possible graves. The only reason we do that for so long is because both of us know deep down that one or both of us could die here. Just thinking about it makes me almost want to laugh and cry.

There is one place where no teen, kid, or adult wants to die – a school. In this case we wouldn't just die; we would reanimate into a dead corpse, craving human flesh. We would just roam the halls forever, just waiting for an unlucky human to bite into.

Before those thoughts could bring down my mood, I shake them out of my head. We turn around and open the double doors and walk back into the school that should have killed us a long time ago.

The doors we walk into open to the front office, which consists of a bar-type circular desk and chairs by the window. Behind the desk is the principal's office, the very place where a nice man was eaten alive by monsters that I've known how to kill ever since I started to be friends with John.

All we can see from the desk is a blood splattered wall. The only reason we don't go into the principal's office is because I really don't think we are scared enough to kill my past principal yet. Yet. When we pass the office, we walk into the sophomore hallway. The sophomore hallway is just another hallway, except for the fact that there is paper strewn as if a tornado charged through the school with lockers left open, like in a post-apocalyptic movie or something.

The only other thing that is out of the ordinary, are the faint moans. I whisper to John.

"Mane, we might be in a little trouble." He nods and pushes a finger to his lips. "We need to go to the library and plan there." He starts walking towards the stairs. I follow him with bat, like a sword in the attack position.

. . .

"Oh mama, I'm in fear for my life from the long arm of the law."

"Lawman has put an end to my running and I'm so far from my home."

"Oh mama I can hear you a crying you're so scared and all alone."

"The hangman is coming down from the gallows and I don't have very long."

The beginning of Renegade is all you hear from the both of us. We continue toward the library. After five minutes of walking, we reach the hallway that leads to the library and immediately regret it. The left way of the hallway is filled with zombies devouring the unlucky students that weren't fast enough to escape.

I scan that side of the hallway and hope I don't see Malcobe. I don't. I look to the right and see the library door ajar. I look towards my best friend and see the color in his face drain. He starts for the door and I follow. Everything goes wrong so fast. We are almost to the door, and would have made it without a problem if none of the zombies would have looked up from their dinner.

All it takes is one sniff and a look. The first zombie to look up and see us is wearing a shirt for some show that I saw once at a friend's house. It has a skinny man on it and a word in big red letters, "Bazinga". If that zombie wouldn't have looked at us, we wouldn't have looked like Indiana Jones running down the hill.

We sprint to the library the moment we hear the clumsy footsteps and a moan of a new kind of death. John is the first in the library.

He almost slams the heavy wooden door on me. Once he closes the door, we see the librarian banging on the book room door. I look to John and I motion to the door.

I hold the bat in a defensive position and John takes the lead. John touches the librarian's shoulder, and she slowly turns toward us. Her eyes are pale as a whale's belly. She hasn't decayed yet but I can see the hunger in her eyes.

Before John can even get out the way, the librarian lunges at him. He reacts in a way I have never seen before. His fist flies through the air to connect with the librarian's jaw. She doesn't even fall down; all she does is look dazed. I pull John behind me and swing the bat for the head of the undead librarian.

They say you never forget your first kill, and now I know why. I hit her in the head in the temple, and that knocks her against the wall. She hits the wall and I swing again, this time at the legs.

I hear a cracking sound and she hits the ground face first. I lift the bat over my head, and bring the aluminum cylinder down with a force of hatred, fear and anger. I splinter the skull. Black blood coats me and the wall. I drop to my knees and I fall on the floor. The bat rolls out of my hand.

CHAPTER 2

FELIX

I really hate bad dreams.

I hear dozens of low moans and a voice I know. The voice sounds scared.

"Wake up, Mane, we have to get out of here." I feel shaking through my entire body. A boy's voice is the only thing I hear beside the moaning and a crying baby. It takes me a minute to realize that the boy's voice is John, and the crying baby is Elliot. I try to open my eyes.

When I actually do open my eyes, I find myself in a library. I am caked with black blood lying next to a dead zombie. I can see the smashed brain inside the destroyed skull. A small puddle of blood is slowly leaking out of the smashed head. Instantly it hits me, all of it. How I killed the librarian, and how I blacked out. I walk over to John with a searing headache.

I say in a raspy voice. "Dude, my head feels like a jack hammer." He doesn't respond. I keep walking, the headaches getting worse. Before I get within ten feet of John, the headache turns into a disease. When I start to hurt, John starts to hurt. The pain is more than I can handle. When I get to him, I put my hand on his shoulders. I pull on his shoulder and he drops to his knees, yelling "You did this to us."

His face is pure torture. Trinity walks through the door with a face of pure disgust. She walks past, the pain filling her. Her beautiful face is pale with dread. Her sparkling green eyes are filled with hatred and torture. I try to say something but my throat is clogged with the welling sensation to burst into tears. I try to move towards her to hug her but I am pulled to my knees. I try to fight it, but as the girl I learned how to write poetry for gets closer, I start to choke.

When she finally stands in front of me all the air in my body is gone, but I won't die. The spirit of death won't consume me. I have to see the girl I love, kill me slowly. Before it all ends, I see a smile on her face. She starts to laugh. I can't say anything, all I can do is sit there and watch her laughing as I die a slow, torturing death. The edges of my vision turns black. I know I am about to be in the inky abyss.

All the energy in my body is drained; every ounce of happiness is washed away with the torturous stare of the girl I love. Before I pass into the inky void of death, Trinity puts a hand under my chin and lifts my head to where I can see her.

"You pathetic little boy. You couldn't help us; you couldn't even get out of the school without passing out. How did you think this apocalypse was going to play out? Did you think that you could lead us into safety? You failed us Felix. You failed me. You let me die. YOU LET US ALL DIE!"

Her voice is filled with icy hatred. I can see her eyes fill with the same cold feeling. With that I feel the inky darkness fill my veins, and it consumes me. I feel the icy touch of death's hands. They take me with no remorse. The last thing I hear is the icy laughter of the girl that I love. After I die, I burst out of the dream and open my eyes.

. . .

When I wake up from the dream, I am in the back of a car with a baby bag and a baseball bat. I instantly know whose car I am in. I don't talk, all I do is stare out of the window, until someone looks back to see me awake.

The person who looks at me is someone I haven't seen in a long time, Everet Summits. He used to be my friend until he moved away three years ago. He is the only person who knows my secret.

"Felix, how's it going?"

"Well, you know Everet, I just killed my first zombie, ran from zombies, passed out, and I just woke up from the worst nightmare I have ever had in my life. Oh and I just saw the guy who I thought moved a long time ago. So I want to say life is going pretty well."

I have a sarcastic tone to my voice. After a few seconds of awkward silence, John breaks it.

"So, half the world was right when the first news started covering the virus outbreaks. Plus, the good news is we were right. But the bad news is that half the world was right."

He pauses for a second to catch his breath. "Now we need a plan of action. No prisons or towns in Georgia or farms, that's where half the population is going."

I sit up. "John, we have to find a place to stop. I have a really bad headache and my house is about half the town over, and if you haven't noticed the traffic is horrible. Plus, you know as well as I do that the worst day of the outbreak is the first day."

"Yeah I know but, we sent the rest of the group to your house and I live by you so my house is out. Malcobe?"

Malcobe starts to talk but Everet cuts in. "Uh guys, my family just bought a house here about a month ago and we are close to it and considering the traffic, the rest of your group is probably close too." We all sit and think about what he says. Through all of this talk, Malcobe is quiet, which is unusual. I finally say what is on John and Malcobe's mind. "Where is it?"

"It's across the street from the air base, and that gas station with the sub shop in it." We nod.

Then I say, "I'm going to call Trinity and tell her that the plan is changed, we are going to Everet's house."

I pull my phone out of my pocket and I call Trinity. It rings for a few seconds, then she picks up. "Felix, are you okay?"

"Yes, Trin I am fine but there has been a slight change of plans. We aren't going straight to my house; we are going to a house that is across from the base."

"Is it purple?"

I ask Everet, and he nods. "Yes. How'd you know?"

"Because we are stuck in traffic in front of it, but we can't get out."

"Why?"

Trinity pauses and I hear a low moan, then a gunshot. "Well, Felix, we are surrounded by half the military from the base waging a war on the undead. Long story short, the military isn't winning."

Now it is my time to pause. I pull the phone from my ear and ask Malcobe, "How far are we?"

"Felix, we are about two minutes away."

"Can we make it in less time if we walk?" I look out the window and my question is answered for me. Dozens of people are running down the lanes panicked. Some of them are trampling others, others are getting eaten by zombies. I look at the car next to us, and what I see scars me more than all my nightmares combined.

A newly reanimated woman is feasting on her son. She starts by biting through the stomach, and eating the skin. Then she moves to the insides. Lifting bloody parts to her mouth. Eating with a hunger that will never be filled. Blood coats her hands like icing. The whole time her son is still alive. His eyes are full of terror unlike anything I have ever seen before.

He's crying and his fire of life is dancing its last dance. He stares at me until he draws his last breath. She pulls more and more from him. She can't get enough. Devouring her son. Blood spilling from the opened stomach like a river. A Blood stain hits the window as I look away. Malcobe answers my question.

"Yeah." I nod and try my hardest to keep from crying, as I put the phone back to my ear and say with a shaky voice.

"Just stay right there. Please just stay in the car. Please."

Trinity's voice is the same as it always. "Ok."

"Trinity promise me that you will stay in the car."

"I promise."

"See you soon." She hangs up and I put my phone back in my pocket.

"Malcobe, we're getting out and walking to Everet's house." I say these words without my usual happy tone. No one says anything. I have to wait for somebody to open the back door before I get out. Malcobe opens the door to get the baby bag and I grab the bat.

I get out and a wave of grief hits me. All the people dying because they were shocked and scared. All of them are either too slow or too weak to kill the reanimation of a person who was too slow or too scared.

John puts a hand on my shoulder, and I almost hit him with the bat.

"Whoa, dude watch out." I rub the back of my neck. "Sorry, I guess I am just on edge and worried about Trinity."

He starts to smile. "All you have to do is keep running towards your dreams."

"Really? Come on. I fell one time in a race, and you will never let it go."

"Still funny two years later."

I instantly get back my usual optimistic tone, as I walk away from John.

"Malcobe, we need to get going. The rest are trapped in the car because the military started to 'contain the outbreak'. So we need to go now." I take point and we all start walking but, it is like running through mud. The crowd pushes us towards the house, but slowly. After about two minutes we make it to the house and I instantly see why Trinity is trapped. The military didn't even stand a chance. It was a slaughter. The zombies were like a flood and the military was like a wall made of sticks. There were more zombies feasting, than I ever wanted to see. I try not to think about all the dead people and turn to the rest.

I motion for everybody to crouch and be silent, but that is pretty hard since we have a baby and a crowd is rushing to the madness. I try to whisper at first but the surrounding barrage of gunshots, screams, and moans make it pretty hard.

"Ok group, you see that purple house over there by the funeral home?" They all nod and keep their attention on me.

"We need to get there, but the thing is that the rest of the group is in one of these cars. Malcobe, you need to get to the house and see if there is anybody there that can help us. Everet and John, you two are coming with me; we are going to get the rest, even though I am the only one with a weapon." When I pause they keep looking at me.

"If anybody or anything comes up to you, maneuver around them. Just remember not to get in a fist fight with the military, and if you see any weapons pick them up. We will need them when we have to secure a base." They all nod and I stand up.

"Malcobe, when I say three you sprint for the purple house and don't look back." She nods and hugs me. I hug her back. I say three and the plan snaps into action. Malcobe sprints to the house with her baby Elliot. The rest of us run right into the action. It takes a few seconds but we find the car. When I see it I almost drop the bat. There is a ring of zombies around it and most of the zombies are the people that we saw on the way here.

I look back at my two companions. "You know this is stupid right?" John knows all about my stupid plans. He also knows that most of them work.

"We need a distraction and we need a fast one. Did anybody actually pick up a gun or anything?" They both say no. I start to rub my thigh. That's what I do when I can't think of a way to get out of a mess or if I am nervous. And so far seeing the military fail at containing a mass outbreak of undead people wasn't helping. I start to pace around.

"Alright who wants to be the distraction? You have to be fast." Both of them just stare at me. John starts to speak up.

"I have a lot to lose but that's not what is keeping me from running and getting a lot of zombies off of my friends. The thing that's keeping me from doing that is the zombie right behind you." I turn around and sure enough there is a zombie right behind me. I step back and it advances. I swing the bat and smash the zombie on the side of the skull. I say some really, really bad words under my breath.

The zombie falls and the blood starts to make a puddle. The zombie has a military uniform on. I turn the now dead zombie over to look at the name tag and see if he had anything useful on him.

His nametag reads "Corporal Jenings." I start to search his pockets. I find a little pocket knife, a wallet, and a picture of his wife. I try not to focus on the picture. I put all of these things in my pockets. Then I see on his belt a nine millimeter standard military issue hand gun. Along with two full clips of ammunition. I take off his belt and holster. I toss the belt to John and hand him the gun. "Guys I might have an idea and this plan will most likely get something killed."

. . .

I start rubbing my thigh again. "Ok so there are about five, maybe six, zombies around the car that just so happens to be the car we need to get to. So the plan is going to revolve around how many we can draw from the car. Now we have a gun and John has the best aim because his dad is a collector. So John you get the gun. The gun is only if the plan hits the fan, which it most likely will." I stop and two pairs of eyes are staring at me and in that moment I realize I don't like to be a leader but someone has to do it.

"Now, Everet would you like the knife or the bat?"

"I would rather the bat." I toss him the bat and I almost wish I didn't after I get a better look at the knife. The knife is a standard pocket knife. The blade is about three inches long, stainless steel. The other thing the knife had was an engraving. "Happy birthday." I really hate today.

"John, how many bullets does the clip have?"

He unlocks the clip. "Uh, about ten."

"We might just survive this one then." John cocks the gun. "Uh, Felix why don't we just kill all the zombies? I mean I have ten bullets more than enough for five zombies."

"Well, if you want to just go and ruin a complicated plan and just shoot…" Before I can even finish my sentence five shots ring out. Each one of them making some kind of contact with its target. I see at least three of them fall like a sack of bricks. The rest look at us and start shambling towards us.

"Really, John? I mean I had a perfectly good plan to lead them away from the car. And for you and Everet to rescue the group."

"You're just jealous that I saved them faster than you."

"No, John, aren't you like changed, I mean you just killed two zombies. Two dead things that just moments earlier used to be people."

"The key words in that sentence are used to."

I can't help but smile. "Let's just get inside." Everet and I rush towards the shambling dead. Three zombies, two teenagers. I look back at John.

"Dude, take the third one out, lead it towards you." In the back of my mind I keep thinking about how this is all happening. The apocalypse, worldwide disease and zombies. But the biggest thing is that I am leading people into danger. I know John will follow me into hell and back but why is Everet here? He probably still trusts me.

Behind me, between the gunshots and moans, I here John shouting at the third zombie. When he finally gets that it doesn't hear him he runs toward it. I run towards mine. I notice the decay process hasn't taken affect yet on the zombies, usually from what I know it happens in about a week after reanimation. So in about a week all the undead soldiers will be starting to decay. This means after the first month all the undead will start to decay.

I hoped this won't get me killed. The zombie I have to kill is about six feet tall. While I am only about five ten, I try to think of the best battle plan in this situation. I charge at the deadly monster with the three-inch knife in my right hand. I don't come up with a plan in time, so I improvise.

I kick the tall zombie in the knee and the monster falls forwards. I hear a cracking noise, and the diseased monster hits the ground like a lead ball. Its head hit the ground and I hear a moan. I stand over the monster, and I put the knife in both hands and raise my hands over my head. Then, I thrust the knife with all the fear and anger I have in my body. The knife connects with the back of its head and a geyser of blood travels up the knife. I step back and look to Everet.

I start walking towards the car, the knife still in my hand. The adrenaline is still flowing. When I get to the car I knock on the window and step back. The door opens and a tan girl with ebony hair launches like a spring. I drop the knife and I am forced to the ground. Her arms rap around me like a clamp. She doesn't even care about the monster blood on my clothes from the librarian. I close my arms around her. She doesn't kiss me though. We disconnect and a smile is on her face, but she is on the verge of tears.

"I told you that I would help you out, Trinity." Her smile widens.

"If you ever pull a stunt like that again Felix, I might have to kill you." Now it's my turn to put a smile on my face. I stand up and I reach my hand out to help Trinity up. "Now let's go girly, I have a searing headache." I put my arm around her and the rest of the group follows us as we rush towards the house of the person that knows my secret.

. . .

Once in the house, we see Malcobe. She is sitting down and talking with a man. They notice us when we enter the kitchen. It is like any other kitchen, colored red.

"Malcobe, we need to make a plan, and the plan has to be good because we can't stay here long. We might be able to stay here for a day but the soldiers are losing. I really hate to say that but it is true. Plus, I have to get my stuff from my house and I need to get some clean clothes, because I look like I just bathed in the blood of my enemies."

The man she was talking to, who I recognize as Everet's dad, says to Everet. "Go, get Felix some clothes." Everet just nods and walks out of the kitchen. Martini looks at me and looks at Malcobe.

"Now, tell us all what happened when we left." Before I can begin to explain, Everet walks in with a pile of neatly folded clothes. He hands them to me and directs me to where the bathroom is. I thank him and head off to the bathroom.

When I get there I lock the door and relieve myself, then I take off my shirt and look in the mirror. What I see in the mirror will probably change. I see a scared, bloody, fifteen year-old boy, who was thrust into a world of death and darkness. I will see a lot of things, blood and gore but a lot of sadness and death. Then I am ripped from my thoughts and back to the start of the apocalypse by my phone ringing. The person calling is my cousin, Alex. I answer and she I hear the fear in her voice.

"Felix, you were right about the strange cannibalistic acts on the TV. I was at swim practice, and one of the other swimmers was acting all sick and then died. She came back to life and bit the coach." She pauses. "I… I ran home, and Tim was waiting at the house by the garage." She finally stops and I have my turn to talk. I put the phone on speaker before I start to talk. "Alright, Alex were you bit?"

"No. neither was Timmy." I sigh a breath of relief.

"Ok, you have to stay there and text your parents and text Uncle Scott. Give the phone to Timmy." Timmy is Alex's boyfriend. I really don't like him.

"Timmy, I really don't like you, but I have to trust you till I get to you. Now I need you to do something that I better not regret." I pause to put on the shirt, and the shorts that Everet gave me.

"You have to protect her. She and I are really close. If she dies, I will never forgive you, and if I find out you left her to die I will kill you with a tennis racket. Are you following me so far?"

"Yes." I can hear in his voice that he is more scared of me than the zombies.

"Ok. You can call your parents after I am done, but until my uncle gets there you are in charge. Please don't make me regret this. Now, find weapons and keep Alex calm. Let her call or talk to as many friends as she needs to. I will be there in a few weeks. Now, Alex's house will be your base for the next two weeks. In those two weeks, don't leave the house unless under siege or for food. If you move to another house let me know."

"Now give the phone to Alex." While he is giving the phone to Alex, I put on my shoes.

"Alex, I will be there in two weeks, tops. I promise. I will be there. Let Uncle Scott know I will be there. See you soon older cousin." I can hear her crying now.

"See you soon baby cousin." She hangs up the phone, and I realize I am also about to cry. I totally forgot about her and Texas. I don't know if I can even get there in a few weeks. I start rubbing my thigh. I take a deep breath, and think about now. Now I have to get my friends to safety. I take another deep breath and walk out the door, down the hallway and back to my group.

. . .

When I get back to the kitchen I realize my headache is worse now. I walk to Everet and whisper to him.

"Uh, dude I forgot your dad's name. What is it?" He whispers back.

"His name is Michael." I nod and walk back over to Trinity, who is standing behind Malcobe holding the baby. I turn to Michael.

"Do you have anything for a headache, like aspirin?" He nods and moves over to the cabinets by the stove. He opens one and pulls a bottle out and tosses it to me. I thank him and take one pill and toss it back to him and he sits back down.

"Ok, guys now we need a plan, and it has to be good, because I haven't heard any gunshots for a while." I look around the table, and all of them are staring at me with a kind of respect.

"My cousin called me while I was in the bathroom. I need to go get her, but right now we need to get to each of our houses and get our stuff, find a base, then I will get her." I look around the room.

"Now I know we all had our own individual plan for the apocalypse, but right now, we need to find a place to go that has a fence or walls, and other stuff. I mean we all planned this haven't we?" I am about to rub my thigh again but Christian pipes in.

"How about the school? It has a fence, places to hide in case of a siege, and fields for farming." All of us are looking at him. I stand up straight.

"Good idea Christian, but it is overrun by zombies, and…" My face goes slack and I almost shout eureka.

"You're right. That is a perfect place and after we get all of our individual stuff from our houses, we can take the place back but we will have to wait at least a week before we go take it over. In the mean time I can go and get my cousin. But I will get her after we find a temporary place to set up." We all have a grin on our faces.

"Ok guys, we will stay here for three days and then take two cars to the houses we need to go to then meet back here. Agreed?"

Everybody nods their head. All of us have a grin on our faces when we file out of the kitchen. I go to the living room and after a few seconds my grin is gone. I just can't help but think I made a mistake trusting Timmy. But I realize something. I realize what I already knew and feared. You need people.

CHAPTER 3

JOHN

The first day we stay at Evert's house. We all rest and listen to the moans that get less and less frequent. The undead are leaving the area to fulfill the hunger that plagues them. The gunshots from the military also stop. Felix is distant the first day. He also keeps looking at his phone every twenty minutes. His face has the touch of sadness and worry on it. All he can think about is his cousin.

Nobody talks to him that first day, not even Trinity. Other than that, the day flies by like a dream. At night we all get to our sleeping arrangements. I bunk with Evert, Felix, and Christian in Evert's room. In the living room Michael, Tom, and Billy sleep there.

In the spare room bunks Emily and Trinity, and in the most comfortable room (the master bedroom or Michael's room) bunks Malcobe with Elliot and Martini. Elliot is sleeping in a crib that Michael and his late wife purchased for their unborn child.

We all don't sleep well the whole time we are there, none of us, not even Evert and Michael. It is the worst for Felix. None of us get any sleep with Felix in the room. Felix keeps waking up in the middle of the night, screaming, but his screaming doesn't wake the whole house, just us. When I try to ask him about his nightmares all he says is that he keeps dreaming about how he would hurt the people he loved and got the people who trusted him with their lives, killed. He also says it is the same dream over and over again.

After he says that he goes back to sleep. It is a continuous cycle throughout the night. But in the morning he is back to his old self. He is optimistic and he laughs at stupid jokes and he won't shut up. But at night the nightmares continue. On the last day he is still optimistic. When we leave for our houses he is still optimistic, but I can see the terror in his eyes. That's all I can see. But he never lets the terror show. Trinity also sees it. She smiles at him but when she looks at me, her expression says she is worried. I am worried but I can't talk to Felix. Not yet at least.

We spend an hour walking from Evert's house to the neighborhood where the rest of us live. We can't take a car because of the ocean of dead cars. We also can't make any noise because of the amount of undead that is roaming the almost dead town. We don't see that many humans, but who we do see are people who we know would get us killed so we avoid them.

None of us talk that much, that is until we get to the neighborhood where most of us lived. The first house we go to is Felix's. The neighborhood doesn't look that good either. Most of the houses have broken windows and cars are crashed into light poles.

When we get to Felix's house we split into two teams to make this faster. I am in the group with Trinity, Felix, and Malcobe with Elliot, Emily, and Tom. The rest go with Martini to go to their houses. We tell them to meet here when they are done. They say ok and run off to their houses. Felix gets in front of the group and looks at each of us.

"This isn't going to be as quick as we think it will be. We will go through my house, John's house, Malcobe's house, Christain's house, Trinity's house, and finish it off with Emily's house." He stops for what seems like a long time. I can still see the terror in his eyes. He has to be afraid of his dreams, and he might think they will come true. He starts to rub his thigh but he stops before he speaks.

"Does everybody have a weapon?" We all nod our head and still look at him.

"Now let's get this over with." He turns around and walks toward his house. Felix's house looks like a typical two story house on the outside. Its painted gray with white windows. As we walk towards the porch I look towards Malcobe. "Have you noticed Felix's weird behavior?"

"John, all I know is that we might have had plans for this apocalypse and trained physically but you can never train yourself for something like this mentally. It's the same thing with solders going to war. They train for physical combat but they will never be ready for the mental torment they will endure. All they think about is survival in combat and that's all they see is survival and death."

I look at her while walking, and thinking about what she just said. I play and toy with that comment. I know I will never forget that. But, all I can hope to do is be prepared enough to protect the people I love. I push that thought in the back of my mind when I walk up the stairs to Felix's porch. I ready my weapon when Felix touches the doorknob. He looks back at us.

"Guys, my bat will not do much good when I open the door. I will back up and will help you anyway I can. I am going to ask only one time. Are you ready?" He looks at each of us. We all nod at him and ready ourselves for whatever is behind that door.

He turns his attention back to the door. His legs are facing to the right so when he moves he moves away. His left hand is on the door and his right is on the bat. His left hand turns the doorknob and opens the door. When he opens the door, we are met with a decomposing smell. I look at Felix and his cockiness is gone. Instead of terror covering his face, sadness takes its place. His eyes still have the look of terror in them.

I switch my gaze to Trinity. She looks like she just saw her parents die. Felix then steps in front of the dark void.

"Guys, I might have to kill my parents. At least I don't have to kill my mom after she gave birth." All of us just look at him with a small smile. None of us have anything to say, he starts to rub his thigh before he starts talking again.

"Before we walk into this I just want to tell you my secret. My real mom abused me when I was kid. She was an alcoholic." His voice breaks after he says that. He doesn't cry.

"The abuse only stopped because when my grandparents died. My grandfather made my dad promise that my dad will be a better father than he was. So he divorced my mom and got married to Janet." A tear rolls down his cheek. All I can think is that it won't be the last tear.

The terror in Felix's eyes isn't there anymore. Instead it's replaced with sadness. All of just stay quiet but I know it would be an awkward stay here for a week. He wipes his face and then says one sentence that I will never forget.

"My dad used to tell me that the only way to survive in the world is to focus on something good in the world and fight for that." Then, after what feels like forever he looks at all of us.

"Now, let's get this over, I still might have to kill Janet, and my dad, but at least I will never have to see my mom ever again." He turns around and walks into the house. All of us just follow him, and as I close the door behind me, I realize that all of us will follow him through hell and back.

. . .

Felix's house is just the same as most of the houses in the neighborhood, classic with its own flair, but what really sets it apart are the posters of 80s movies. I mean they have all of them but there is one that I haven't seen yet. It has five teenage kids in front of a white background and the title is in big red letters. The teenagers are all from different backgrounds. The backgrounds look to be a brain, an athlete, and a basket case, a princess, and a criminal. The poster reminds me of when Felix gave Tom Donavan a copy of the movie for his birthday.

That is just one of the many movie posters around the living room. But all I can think about is the putrid smell. I know someone is dead. Felix points to a hallway to the left and he moves there and pushes the light switch. Blood covers the hallway and the smell gets worse. It looks like a morgue. Felix just keeps walking down the hallway to the stairs and then to his room.

When we get to his door the door is caked in dried blood. I try to look at Felix but all I can see is his back. But, I know what he is thinking. All he can probably think about is the faces of his dead parents. I know I will probably feel the same way in an hour or so. Felix turns around and looks at Trinity, then the rest of us.

"I thought I was ready for this, I had a plan, but I can't do this. If I go into that room and I have to kill my parents…." I can hear the breaking in his voice. The brave boy that was there, is now gone.

He is shaking, his whole body is filled with the terror that used to be in his eyes. He just looks around and all of our weapons are down. The pistol I am holding is on safety for the first time since I got it. He stops shaking and tears flood down his face.

"I can't do it, and if I can't do this, then I won't survive." He stops crying and I look at Trinity. She's on the verge of crying to, so is Malcobe. At that moment I know this is going to be bad. I can feel that somebody here has to speak up and I know I am the one. I click the safety back into fire.

"Felix I have known you for long enough to know, that you have always been the person to survive. I mean you survived childhood abuse and you turned out a good guy, plus you have a girlfriend. I also know you're one of the toughest guys I have met. I mean you have been run over by a golf cart." Felix makes a smile when I say that.

"If anyone of us can survive this apocalypse it is you. I know why you can't do this, I mean, I will probably have to the same thing in an hour or so and I am not looking forward to it. None of us are and if you think that any of us are looking forward to killing the people who cared for us, then you won't make it."

They all just stare at me. I look at Felix.

"Now open that door and get it over with. I want to know if I get bit, I can trust that my best friend will be able to kill me after I have turned for like five minutes."

Felix just laughs and reaches for the door knob.

"Same thing as we did when we got into the house, oh and John I will kill you after five minutes." I give him a smile and raise the pistol to where I can shoot it. Trinity and the rest are behind me except for Malcobe. She is away from this so that the baby doesn't cry. He looks at us and we all nod back. He turns the door knob and moves out of the way.

. . .

I walk in after Felix opens the door. I get to just behind the doorway before a stick hits my arm. I look to the right and almost shoot when I see the familiar face. I put the pistol back to safety and put the gun in the holster. The man and I just laugh. The rest of the group files in after me when they hear the laughter. When the man sees Felix, Felix rushes the man and almost knocks him over. They disconnect and the father and son are both almost crying.

"Dad, where's Janet?"

Felix's dad's smile just plummets to a frown. He puts his hand on Felix's shoulder.

"I had to kill her son. It was the only way. She got bit by a zombie." Felix's smile turns into a frown to.

"Was it quick and easy? Did she suffer?" Felix's dad just stares into his son's eyes. That moment I can see Felix loved his step-mom. He loved her more than I could ever understand because my parents never got divorced.

"No Felix, she didn't suffer. I stabbed her in her head." The last word is said with a twinge of terror. I know I will probably have to say the same thing and say it in the same way. That's what scares me. I know every time I say that it will get more common and it will be easier. It will be easier to tell people that their loved ones died, but the thing about dying in this new word is they will probably not die without suffering.

All of us will have to say it one day. All of us will also have to kill something to survive in this world and that is what scares me the most. Then, I'm snapped back into the present by a deep moan, and a fall. I turn around, and see a shambling figure moving up the stairs. Felix looks at his dad. "What did you kill mom with?"

"I killed her with a knife you bought when we went to Gatlinburg." Felix nods.

"Where is it?"

"It's on the other side of the bed. Why you have a bat?"

"I like to use my own stuff, plus I mean it is my knife."

His dad just looks at him with a face that looks like he is about to laugh, but he's not. Felix just walks around the bed, and bends over and pulls a knife in a sheath that is about thirteen inches, in total, and the blade is eight and a half inches. Felix looks at me and says.

"Is it up the stairs yet?" I look back at the stairs.

"No. I would advise to fight it once it gets up the stairs." He looks at me when I say that and smiles.

"John, I just found out that my step-mom just died, and I am mad. Do you think that I am going to think rationally?"

"No. Felix I don't. I would do the same thing." He nods and walks toward the door. I look at Trinity and I know she is just stunned. The rest just funnel out to the top of the stairs and I move towards Trinity.

"You know he will never be the same again right?"

"John, none of will be the same way after we visit our own houses. Some of us might not be as lucky as Felix." I look at her before I speak again.

"What do you mean as lucky?"

"He didn't have to kill any of his parents." That hits me harder than anything that has happened in the last few days. I move to Emily, and I take her hand in mine. She looks at me and we stare at each other's eyes for what feels like forever.

"Emily, Felix will never be the same anymore, and the same thing will probably happen all of us. We will probably have to kill more than just dead things, and I know you know this, but can you promise me that you won't look at me as an animal; No matter what I do?" It feels like an hour before she answers; and I like that, it means she had to think about the answer and not say what I want to hear.

"John, you must be crazy if you think that I will look at you as an animal."

I smile at that and kiss her. We are snapped back into the grim reality when we hear a metal penetrating bone sound. We both look to the stairs and watch as Felix pours all of his grief into the knife. He keeps slamming the knife in and out of the skull. His dad pulls him away from the dead monster. When he pulls him away tears stream down Felix's face. His eyes are red and puffy and when his dad touches his shoulder he says one thing.

"None of us will get used to the feeling of grief." His dad looks at him and nods.

"You're right Felix. But we have to push it down and keep going. No matter what." Felix nods and hugs his dad. He cries in his dad's arms and I look at Trinity. She looks as if she is about to cry. When Felix stops crying, he starts to walk up the stairs with his dad following. Before his dad walks back into Felix's room I look at him and ask him something.

"What is your name?"

"John after all these years you never learned my name?" I nod and he answers my question.

"My name is Jack." He looks away and he walks back into the room, while we all fill in.

. . .

When he gets back into the room Felix grabs a back pack from his closet and starts to put all of his gear and some other clothes. His gear consists of a couple of knifes, duct tape, books, deodorant, a belt, and some other things. When Felix gets to his bookshelf I step back and almost trip over Jenny, Felix's guitar, and I pick it up, and smile.

"Felix, are you taking Jenny?" Felix, stops and smiles at me.

"Yeah, I am. But can you carry it till we get to the car?" I nod and pick it up. Finally, when Felix finishes, he throws his dad a duffle bag.

"Dad, when we go down stairs I need you to put food and water in there and unlock the doors to your car."

Jack nods and we all file down the stairs, except for Felix. He stays behind, and I notice this and I stay behind with him.

"I am sorry. About your step-mom, but you have us. And when you have us you're never alone."

Before I can continue Felix stops me. He just looks at me and looks at me with a steely gaze.

"John there is only one thing we have now, and that's people. Now go wait by the door while I take one last walk around my room." I

I nod and walk to the door. When I get to the door way I watch as he picks up the various objects that fell on the floor. When he finishes with that he walks back to the door and looks around. I know this must be hard for him. After, a few seconds he says something.

"Well this is it. I knew I would have to leave this place someday. I just didn't know when." With that he turns off the light and closes the door, which also closes his childhood.

. . .

"John, you know that the plan to go get Alex, is the most insane thing I will probably ever do? Right?" I nod, and look at him.

"Felix, you know that being friends with you is the most insane thing I have ever done, right?" We both smile at that as we walk down the stairs and our smiles get bigger when we see Trinity and Emily in the kitchen, helping Jack and the others get the canned goods and water into the big duffle bag. Before we could say anything to them, we hear moans. We all look at the back door. On the back door there is a window. We see shadows and hear the moans and the group at the pantry looks at us, and Felix motions us to get down, which we do.

I look at Felix and whisper, "We need to get out of the house and go to my house; especially since we have a baby."

He nods and starts to crawl over to the other group and I put the guitar on my back and join him. We stop half way when something starts to bang against the door. Felix looks at me and we go faster.

We stop again when the moans get louder and closer and the banging against the door becomes more and more frequent.

Bang Bang

Bang

I look at Felix and we move even faster, until finally we get there. Emily hugs me, and a bead of sweat falls trickles down my forehead and onto the floor.

Bang

Bang

Bang

Bang

Bang

Felix gets on his knees and looks at the group. "Guys, we need to get out of here and into another house. There is no need for silence we need to get out of here." Felix stands up all the way and takes his knife out of his belt.

"Now, Dad zips up that duffel bag and gets a kitchen knife. We are leaving."

Bang

Bang

Jack nods and I wrap my hand around Emily's.

"Emily, hold onto your knife. You cannot die; I won't let that happen." She nods and let's go of my hand, and tightens her grip on her knife and I tighten my grip on the bat. We all stand up and I stand move towards Felix.

Bang

Bang

Bang

Bang

Bang

Bang

Bang

I look at the back door and the hands of mindless monsters smack against the glass. Then, I notice a small crack getting bigger and bigger. I look at Felix and whisper into his ear.

"Felix, we are going to my house but we will need to take a car." He nods and looks at the rest of the group.

"Dad you need to get the car keys we are going to John's house." Malcobe peeps in after that.

"How are we going to meet up with the others?"

"Crap you're right I don't know. Maybe…" A shattering sound fills the room and I look at the door. Decaying monsters have finally broken through the glass and are desperately scratching at nothing and looking for contact with the warm flesh of a living breathing thing.

"No time now. We need to leave now." Felix turns and we all follow. We follow him through the living room, through the front door, and then finally into the drive way where two cars are parked. One car is an old beat up suburban that Felix's dad calls "Old Nelly Bell". The other is a small two door Mustang. That just happens to be cherry red.

Jack unlocks the suburban and I open the trunk of the car and put the guitar in it and climb over the back seats and plant myself in one of them. Emily joins me and I wrap my hand around hers and the side doors open and the rest spill in and Felix and Trinity join us. Malcobe is in the passenger seat and Tom joins us too.

Jack starts up the car and puts it in drive as I look back at the house. Zombies spill out the door we came from. There are at least ten in total. I look forward and try to not to think about what could have happened. I look down at my hand that wasn't holding Emily's hand. My knuckles are white and my hand is cramped from clutching the gun.

"Well that was a close one." I say that without even thinking, and Jack starts to laugh. So does Malcobe and the laughter spreads to the rest of us. I don't know why we are laughing but I know that it might be the weirdest moment in my life. I look at Emily and her smile makes me warm in side.

We all stop laughing when Elliot starts to cry. That brings us all back to the black reality in which we have prepared for. I drop the gun and tap Tom on the shoulder.

"We did it man. One house down the rest to go, and after that we will find you a girlfriend." He smiles.

"Yeah, maybe we might just find a random girl on the way to Texas." I smile and sit back, and breathe a sigh of relief. I totally forgot about Texas and how that is probably the Hell that I will follow Felix through. I know all of us will go with him. But the thing that still has me is, what will he do if Alex, isn't there, what if she died? I shake that thought out of my head and look out the window as we approach my house, and I think about how I probably won't be as lucky as Felix.

CHAPTER 4

ALEX

"Timmy I can't do this anymore. It's been a week and my dad hasn't come home; neither has my mom. I can't do this." I say this as I rest in Timmy's arms. He looks at me and starts to open his mouth, but a loud car horn fills the silence. Timmy unwraps his arms and moves towards the window.

"There is a bright orange 1969 Dodge Charger in your drive way. Two people are walking out of it, both of them are blonde and one is a boy and the other is a girl. The boy looks like he is six foot and the girl is smaller." A smile widens on my face.

"Timmy, those are my friends. The tall guy is Austin, and the short girl is Megan. Well they aren't really my friends they are more of Felix's friends." He looks at me with a small smile.

"Let's go meet them." I walk out the room and down the stairs to the back door. I walk out the door and towards the wooden fence that surrounds my back yard. I open the door and rush straight towards them. They open their arms and I close mine around them. We disconnect and I look at them.

"So where have you been?" I smile, as if I couldn't smile tomorrow. Before the two of them could answer, moans break the happiness. I look behind them and see a zombie shuffling along the road. It looks at us and starts to shuffle towards us. The other two people look at the shuffling embodiment of death. I look at Megan, and she looks at Austin.

"I got this, girls." He walks to the car and pulls out a short sword in a sheathe. Austin un-sheathes the sword and tosses the sheathe back into the car.

He charges at the zombie which is slowly advancing toward us. Austin connects with the undead and bulldozes it. The tall boy with the short sword stands over the undead beast. He thrusts the sword over his head and pushes the sword downwards. He drives the sword through the skull of the monster.

Blood bespatters the blade of the sword. Austin pulls the sword up from the decaying monster and he looks up and starts to walk back to us, before anymore can come. I look at Megan.

"Megan, you and Austin need to stay here. Felix is coming to get Timmy and me. He should be coming in a few hours."

"Thanks, Alex. Can you help us get everything out of the car?" I nod and move to the car as Timmy walks outside. He has a kitchen knife in his left hand. He shouldn't have brought that. I look at Megan and she isn't at the car anymore, she's sprinting at Timmy.

Timmy didn't even have time to react before Megan tackles him and the knife clatters on the cement. I run to help him but, Megan is already off of him. Austin laughs behind me, so does Megan. Timmy stands up and anger coats his face.

"WHAT THE HELL WAS THAT FOR!!!!?"

"I thought you were about to attack, I am sorry. Obviously, somebody hasn't been outside of his house before." Megan gets close to Timmy. They might have fought if I didn't push them apart.

"Alex, they aren't staying with us are they."

"Actually Timmy they are. Why do you have a problem with them?" Before, Timmy could answer Austin walks up.

"Alex, calm him down before he gets beaten up by two girls and then gets eaten by the zombies coming up the street." I look at the street and notice the group of zombies shuffling towards us.

"Now, if you three are done talking about your feelings, help me get this stuff out of the car." The three of us start helping Austin get the stuff out of the car. The motley group of terror gets to the car when we get the last bag into the house.

"Let's all just sit down and talk." They all nod and agree with me as we all sit down. Timmy sits next to me, but I can see that the anger still coating his face.

. . .

I am the first to talk after ten minutes of uncomfortable silence.

"So Austin and Megan what happened to you the first few days?" Their smiles fade when they hear that. Megan speaks for them.

"When it all first happened, we were at school…" She breaks out in tears before she cans continue, Austin brings her head to his chest and whispers something into her ear. Austin picks up the story.

"We were at school when the poop hit the fan. We knew that something was going to happen when the government announced a new flu vaccine. My mom said that we needed to leave town and go visit her parents in the country but my dad said it was nothing to worry about." He pauses to fight back tears.

"My dad asked me if I wanted to get the new vaccine, I said no. I told him not to get it because of the news reports on cannibalistic acts and how the people who do these acts can only be killed by a shot in the head, but he didn't listen. He insisted on getting that shot." He stops. I don't know why he stops; it seems like an eternity before he starts again.

"I kept telling him to not to get it but he didn't listen. The day the actual zombie apocalypse started, he turned then. So did my mom. They were sick for a week before they actually died. Both of them had a fever. A really hot fever." I look at him and I can tell by his face that he wasn't prepared to tell us what he did the past week.

"I knew that something bad was going to happen, the day before Monday. That Sunday, the cannibalistic acts were the only thing on the news. I knew that Sunday, that Monday was going to be it." When he says that his voice is weak and small, after a few seconds he continues.

"That Monday is a whole different story. After I got home from school, I called for my parents, but they didn't respond. I walked to their room and when I saw them, I fell to the ground and cried. I cried like I would never cry again.

"When I finally stopped crying, I went to get my phone to call 911. Before, I could I heard a moan, and I ran back to the room and I went to the side of their bed. Before, I could my mom rolled out of bed, literally.

"I went to go help her up, and when I did she tried to bite my hand but I moved it out of the way. My dad rolled out of the bed too and shambled over to me. I ran out of the room and tried to talk to them, but the fact I really didn't want to face was apparent. They were zombies." Now he really looks like he wants to cry. Timmy and I are listening to the story like Austin was a professional story teller.

"When they got out of the room, and shuffled into the living room I had a kitchen knife and was ready to do what no child should ever have to do. I killed my mom first. I knocked her down and stabbed her through the eye. When I killed my dad, I released all of the sadness and anger and any other negative feeling I could muster and embodied it into the knife. I impaled the knife through the skull of my dad."

With that Megan, Austin, and I start to cry. Timmy doesn't cry, but he leaves. He walks into the bathroom and he starts to cry. We all cry. We can't help it; all we could do was cry. I cry because I was lucky enough to not have to kill my parents. I cry because Timmy was lucky. Megan cries because she probably had to kill her parents. The last reason I cry is because, at that moment I know I would never see my parents again.

. . .

When we all finally stop crying, Timmy comes from the bathroom and I see red rings around his eyes. Austin sees it too.

"Looks like somebody didn't want his girlfriend to see him cry."

"I just had to use the bathroom that's all." Now Megan joins in.

"I have seen Austin cry. Alex have you seen Timmy cry?" I look at them.

"No, I have never seen him cry." That really hurts Timmy. He looks at me like it's the first time I hurt him.

"Why are you looking at me like that? You know I have never seen you cry. You know it. In this world now you will have to cry. I know that you know, you will have to cry. I mean you just did in the bathroom. I know that you've see my cry." Austin and Megan look back and forth to me and Timmy. They look like they are watching a ping-pong game.

"Are we really going to fight about this in front of your cousin's weird friends?" When I hear that I stand up from the couch, so does Megan and Austin.

"You're the one that's fighting. I just agreed with Austin, that I have never seen you cry. And to answer your question, we are going to talk about this in front of my cousin's weird friends." I take my gaze from Timmy and look at Austin and Megan.

"No offense." They respond in unison.

"None taken." I can tell they are enjoying this. It takes a minute before the fight gets started again.

"So now you're taking the side of your weird cousin's friends." I just stare at Timmy when he says that.

"First of all, Felix, may be weird, but he would help anybody, unlike you. I mean you brought a knife with you when Megan and Austin arrived."

"There are FLESH EATING MONSTERS OUTSIDE!!!!" From the corner of my eye I can see Austin reach for his miniature sword and Megan reaching for one of her throwing knives. Now Austin steps between Timmy and me.

"Step back man. I can assure you that having a throwing knife in your shoulder doesn't feel good." Megan pipes up, after that.

"Neither does a short roman sword." I look at them, and realize I need a weapon after I am done with this fight.

"Are you threating me? I could take you down within five sec…" Before he can even finish the sentence, Austin launches over the table and tackles Timmy. Before I can push him off of Timmy, Megan holds me from behind. Austin doesn't have his sword, when he tackled Timmy. (Thank God.) Timmy is on the ground under Austin and has his arms protecting his face.

"Really, Tim, you can take us down within five seconds, you can't even take me, you black eyed whore." At this time Austin pulls Timmy's arms apart, and strikes Timmy's nose and I hear a sharp snap. I break out of Megan's arms and throw myself at Austin. This causes Austin to fall sideways in to the cabinet. I help Timmy up, and I yell.

"This is all the time with you. Why do you always think you can beat up everybody? You know I can't. If you try this with Felix, I know he will literally break your arm." He keeps quiet, while I get him into the kitchen so I could stop his nose bleed.

Megan and Austin, walk in a few seconds later. From the counter I could hear Megan whisper "Just be the better man, which I know you are and say sorry, for possibly breaking his nose." I have to bite my lip to keep from laughing. Austin does this and sits at the table, while Megan walks over to help Timmy. I go take a seat by Austin.

"How can you deal with him, Alex?"

"Well I don't tackle him from the other side of the room." Austin laughs at that.

I take my gaze from Austin, and he says something.

"Well that escalated quickly."

I laugh at that. Before I can say anything, Timmy sits up and walks out of the kitchen and up the stairs. Austin yells behind him.

"Looks like he has to get that bundle out of his panties." I punch him in the shoulder and almost go after him. I can see Megan see this.

"Did, you really mean what you said back there after you helped Timmy up from the ground?" I stay quiet for a long moment.

"Yes I did. I know if he acts like that when Felix gets here, he will either get an appendage that no man wants to lose get cut off or Felix will break his arm." With that I get up and head for the couch. I lie down and stretch my body over the long couch.

I get my phone and my ear buds out of my pocket and turn on my music playlist to shuffle as I stare at the ceiling. Looking up at that ceiling, is when everything hits me. The end of the world, never seeing my parents again, my cousin's friend attacking my boyfriend, and the worst, is that I am the reason that my cousin will probably die.

He will probably die on the way here and I will die in this house. Fear and anger seeps into every speck of my body. The two emotions fight at each other like red and blue. But after a while the two enemies coalesce into one. My body screams for something to be done. I just stare at the ceiling and listen to the rhythmic beat of the pop music. The music attacks the united enemies like a good guy to a bad guy.

My eyes start to close as the rhythm fills my body. The dream I have after I close my eyes is all about my parents. I see them try to fight off an enormous group of the flesh eating monsters. They get backed up into a corner and they both drop their weapons and hold hands as they accept the death. The monsters finally reach them and the nightmare still goes on. I yell and cry but the shredding has already begun. Their flesh is torn from the bones like wet paper.

Blood splashes like waves. I can't close my eyes. I am stuck there to watch a death not fit for such good people. Tears sting my eyes. I am finally saved from this nightmare as somebody shakes me awake. I sit up and look at my phone and it says eleven o'clock p.m. I try to say something but somebody has a hand over my mouth. I try to yell but a deep voice speaks right into my ear.

"Shush. Shush. You will be quiet and you won't die. Neither will any of your friends." I nod and he takes his hand off of my mouth and turns me around.

"Walk upstairs and go to your room. Take your friends with you. I will be with you people soon." Before I can even move I hear a voice from behind.

"Let the girl go." The stranger turns around and I feel cold metal being held up to my cheek.

"No you put the long knife down and go up to the room with her. Oh, and tell the midget girl behind me to put the throwing knife down also." I see the glint of a sword and I hear the sound of metal hitting the ground. The metal is gone and I feel a tight metal against my wrists and the man put two other pairs on my friends.

"Now, the brunette will lead you to her room and I will be there shortly." They nod and follow me into my room. On the way to my room I see the front door, it is wide open. We walk up the stairs, and into my room. The man locks the door, and says one last thing before he closes the door.

"You really shouldn't have left the door open. Nor should you have left the light on." I look around, at my friends. When he closes the door, nobody talks. But, we all notice one thing. There were only three captives. Only one of them is a boy.

. . .

"I am not gonna tell you that Felix was right about him. But he was." That is the only thing Austin sys right after, the stranger is gone. I do not cry but what I do is struggle against the hand cuffs. I finally stop and start to talk.

"I really should have listened to Felix. I really should have done a lot of other things. But you know what, I never thought that a zombie apocalypse would happen in the middle of the day. I also never thought my boyfriend would ever leave in the middle of the night. I also never thought that a man would lock me in my room, while he robs my house." I breathe heavily.

Both Austin and Megan stare at me like I am crazy. They both sit silent for a long time.

"Now guys, does anyone here know how to get out of handcuffs?" They both just stare at me again.

"Ok no, so what I have seen on TV, is that you can put your legs through your arms, so you can have your hands out in front of you." I show them first, then they do it, and with that done, I stand up, and look out of the window. A black van is parked outside the front of my house.

I also see several shambling figures, lazily I count twenty in all.

"Ok, so if we make it out of this house and get outside, there are about twenty zombies outside and that is just the front of the house, but there is a black van outside." I stop to look back at the van and I notice more zombies gathering in the front.

"Now the bad news is that we have hand cuffs and no weapons, but our fists and our teeth. Now we have two options. Wait for Felix or take back this house."

"So Alex, when did you become a badass, instead of the girl I saw just a few hours ago?" I think about that question for a long second, and I finally come up with an answer.

"The moment when I realized that I needed a weapon."

The look they give me could make a sad man happy.

"So I take it you're pissed."

"About what?" Now it's my turn to give them a look.

"Well you know the whole boyfriend leaving you and leading to a strange guy coming into your house and putting hand cuffs on your hands and..." I cut Austin off mid-sentence.

"You know what, Austin, maybe you have been right since you got here and maybe Felix has been right since he saw Timmy. But you know what, I have more things to worry about, than a stupid, arrogant, black eyed, son of whore, who leaves his girlfriend at the mercy of this stupid world." I breathe hard. My chest is hurting, and my eyes are glazed with tears. Austin and Megan just stare at me, then, they look at each other. Megan starts to talk.

"You know Alex, maybe we should just sleep the rest of the night, and then escape in the morning. Or we could just wait till Felix gets here. I mean, I know Felix, will come. If he doesn't come, then we could check where he always said he would go if this sort of thing happened." All I hear is her words. I am on the floor crying. I can feel Megan trying to comfort me, but she and I know it won't work.

"Why does this have to happen? Why does Felix have to be so right? I mean he is a crazy person. I should have trusted him. I should have done a lot of things. But you know what, I will probably never do those things now. I will probably die." Those are the last words I say before I cry myself asleep. I don't have any dreams, just blackness. Dark. Inky. Whatever other words you want to call it. The only thing that I will get out of that darkness is that I will not die by the hands of some stranger. I will not die in this house. I will die, after I find Timmy.

"Get up." I feel shaking. My eyes flutter open, and I see the man from last night. His eyes are stormy and filled with lighting. He has a slight stubble, and a scar just above his lip.

"So, glad you kids, didn't decide to try and escape because I had a man right outside your door."

The man is standing in front of the doorway, with three other armed men behind him. I look back at Austin and Megan and Austin has his fists clenched, and is probably thinking of a way to fight off three armed men with hand cuffs on.

"I suppose you are wondering what my name is, and why I locked you in your room. Well before I tell you my personal information, I would like to know what your name is." All three of us just stare at him.

"Ok well, let's start with the brunet in the front." The man looks at me with a smile.

"My name is Sarah Walker." The man laughs at that. His laughter sounds warm and comforting. It's the total opposite of his appearance. I can tell that Austin and Megan are holding in a laugh.

"Ok, well that was not what I was expecting. Usually when I walk into a house and there are three kids and I ask them their names they don't answer. But I could feel a difference in you three. If I didn't know any better I could say the brunet is Alex, and the blonde boy is Austin and the blonde girl is Megan." Our mouths drop open and Austin steps in front of me.

"How do you know?" The man still has the smile.

"My guy heard you three speaking last night. So I assumed, that Austin was a guy's name, and Megan was a girl's name, so was Alex. Am I mistaken?" We all shake our heads.

"So now I assume you three want to hear my name." The three of us just look at the smiling man.

"Well, my name is Zed, but before the world hit the fan, my name was Andy. I had a wife and even a daughter." Now it is Austin's time to ask a question.

"What happened to them?" Zed's smile falters for just a second, when Austin says that.

"Well, we tried to do what you three are doing and wait for somebody to come get us. I had talked to a friend of mine before the whole world hit the fan. That was who we were waiting for. But, some bad people got us first. They were armed. When I say armed I mean really armed." Zed, pulls the chair from my desk and sits down. His smile is completely gone now.

"My friend got to our house about an hour later. My friend was killed. Brutally murdered when he tried to help. The bad guys were mad now. I was tied up and barely conscious, but I could see. I saw what those men did to my daughter. I heard her scream. I heard her cry. I heard the same from my wife. They slowly murdered them. Do you know what it feels like to be helpless?

"It feels like you let them down. I let my wife and child get murdered. Do you know how much I told them to take me instead of them? Do you know what I did to the bad people? I killed them. I only killed them because, they tried to kill me after, and they murdered my family." He pauses and all three of us can hear the pain and anger in his voice.

"They didn't even kill my wife and child all the way. I had to put them down. I had to kill my resurrected child and wife!" He has to calm himself down after that.

"I had to bury them in my backyard. After that I promised to myself that I will never hurt anyone that doesn't deserve it. The only reason I did this to you three is to make sure I didn't have to kill you. All I did was look around the house. Now you may be asking yourself, 'why is a man just going around houses?' Well I am doing this because, I really want to settle down, but I can't till I make sure that the area around where I want to live is safe." Megan and I look at each other, then back at the guy.

"Now I will leave, you three. Oh and we left you three with some weapons and food. Oh and Alex, we left you a special weapon, seeing as how you are the only one without a weapon."

"How'd you know?"

"You didn't pull a weapon on me." The man turns around and walks down the hall. I go after him.

"Zed, wait." He turns around and has the same smile on his face that he did when I first saw him.

"Yes?"

"If you see Timmy, please tell him that I will be coming for him. Where are you staying Zed?" He smiles and laughs.

"You know Alex, when I killed those men, I did it because they needed to die. I killed them because I knew they would do the same thing to other people. I couldn't let them do that to other people. So I will tell this Timmy, what you said, but keep in mind, don't go down the road I did. You will never forget what you did to him if you kill him. Just let it go Alex. He will probably die out there any way. You will probably never see him again in your life, so just let it go and keep that weapon." Now it was time for me to smile.

"Thank you Zed."

"No, thank you." I memorize his face and his smile before, he turns around and walks away. I know that moment I would probably see him again. I know that he will help me if I need it.

"Wait, Zed where will you stay? Just in case I need help." He doesn't turn around this time. All he does is answer the question.

"At the airport." Those are the last words he says, before he leaves the house.

"So, want to go down and see what Zed gave us?" I don't even know that Austin and Megan were behind me.

I turn around and answer Austin's question. "Sure." So we walk down the stairs. Everything is where it was last night, except for, the three bags on the couch. I look at my two companions and they had smiles on their faces. All three of us stand in front of the couch.

"Well let's see what Zed left us." Austin picks up the bag with his name on it. With that Megan and I pick up our bags. I sit on the couch that I slept on last night and see it is filled with food and jackets and some other stuff that will be useful to survive and a note.

But the weapon that Zed told me about is at the bottom. It has a sheathe over it, and it looks as if it was handmade. The cover of the blade has writing on it. The writing is the manufacturer. I take the weapon out of the sheathe it is a hatchet with a hammer on the other side of it. I have never seen one of these before. The handle is a smooth plastic. There is also a belt with a gun holster that I will probably use for holding my hatchet.

In Austin's bag is his gladius, survival things, and a blade sharpener with a cloth to clean it. I put the belt around my waist and put the hatchet in the holster.

"So now that I actually have a weapon, I should probably learn how to use it." So I go outside and open the back gate. Austin and Megan, rush over to me.

"Are you crazy?"

"No, I am just really mad." Megan and Austin just look at each other.

"Sounds like something Felix would say." I ignore that and walk towards the nearest zombie. I rush at it and pull the hatchet with my right hand. I use the hammer part on its knee. The undead nightmare falls to one knee. I turn the weapon around and hold it with two hands and thrust it above my head.

The monster almost gets up but the blade penetrates the skull and splits the brain. The blood doesn't stop at the blade. It geysers up all over my face. I pull the hatchet out of the head and wipe it off with my sleeve. I do the same thing with my face.

"Well someone is really mad." Austin smiles and I look at him.

"Well you know, I am waiting for a hero, one fresh from the fight."

"Well you really don't want one with the name Timmy." I smile at that, and I see the smiles fade off Austin and Megan's face. I see Megan reaching for her throwing knives from her backpack and Austin rushing towards me while reaching for his gladius. I turn around and I see a familiar face except he has an eternal hunger in his eyes.

I say one word that doesn't even matter anymore. "Daddy?" Tears gloss my eyes, and he collapses on me, and I can't reach my hatchet. I clutch his shirt that I bought him for his birthday. The undead monster keeps struggling to kill me. I don't have any strength left and my arms go limp but before the monster can chew my face like taffy, a bullet saves me.

The monster falls on me and I push it off, and I stand up to see who saved me. I should be happy and thankful, but my face goes slack. Austin and Megan get to my side before I could go up and punch him. "I should probably say sorry. Huh?" Before, Austin and Megan could restrain me I sprint towards my savior, and tackle him, his gun slides out of his hand and I sit on top of him.

"You bastard! WHY THE HELL DID YOU DO THAT!!!??" Before he can answer I punch him in the nose, then the gut, then the eye. I keep punching him while the tears fall.

"Answer me!!!!" His blood, is all over me mixing with my dad's. A string of curse words flings out of my mouth. I keep punching him. Megan tackles me and pins me down while Austin lifts up Timmy and whispers into his ear.

"Dude, you don't want to lose your man parts, I would answer her." Timmy's nose and mouth is water falling blood now. He stands up on his own and answers me. "Well, I deserved that." Austin rams the butt of the sword into Timmy's stomach, and he doubles over in pain.

"Well, let me answer you then. I left because, I knew that when we get rescued by Felix, I would probably get kicked out within a week. I don't know why I came back. I saved you didn't I?" Austin hits him again.

"Why did you come back?" Tears stream down my cheeks, and on to the blood soaked ground.

"I came back because I thought I needed you. I really did but now I realize I came back because I left my car keys." Austin slams him across the face, and he collapses like a teen girl meeting a pop star. Austin looks at me.

"What do you want to do with him?"

"Well, I can't just leave him that would be too humane." I wipe my tears and stand up straight.

"Let's get him, I want Felix to deal with him." As if on cue, a black Escalade glides on the top of the street.

“Austin, carry him inside.” Austin brings him inside and Megan stays with me as I go to pick up the gun. I bend down to pick up the gun and I hear moans coming closer. I look up to see a group of zombies making their way to us, the Escalade speeds up. It rams the group and a wave of black blood splashes up from the now dead undead. The now bloodied car stops in front of us and a tall fifteen year-old boy.

“Did you miss me?” I try to smile, but I can’t. What I just did rushes up with me. I just killed my undead father, beat up my ex-boyfriend, and had just almost gotten killed by my monster father. I swim in a sea of emotions and I drown in them. The last thing I see before I hit the pavement is my friend running towards me with a look of fear on his face. My vision goes black and the last thing I feel before I sink into the sea of black emotions and the undead face of my father is my head hitting the hard pavement.

CHAPTER 5

FELIX

"So we should probably talk about who is coming with me?" I look at my group around John's kitchen table. Everet looks up from his book.

"You're actually going to save your cousin? Not to be mean or anything but that seems kind of not safe." I go to respond, but my phone rings. Austin is calling.

"One second, guys we can choose who is going after this phone call." I walk away from the kitchen and go into the living room.

"Austin, I haven't heard from you in a long time."

"Yeah, Felix this isn't the time to be all happy. Alex just fainted and I think one of her friends, just stepped out of a black Escalade. Alex, told me you were coming in a week. It's been a week." My face goes long.

"Yeah, but we had work to do here and we couldn't leave yet. What do you mean somebody got out of a black escalade?" I can hear he is about to answer, but a loud bang goes off in the background.

"Felix, you have to get here. Something is happening outside. Megan got Alex but the person that got out of the Escalade just got shot." I hear another shot and heavy breathing.

"Felix, buddy, when you get hear bring the cavalry. I just…." The line goes dead, so does the power.

"Hello. Hello. Austin are you there?" I take the phone away from my ear and I look at the flashing words on the illuminated screen. 'No connection.' I turn the phone off and head back into the kitchen.

"We need to leave and we need to leave tomorrow morning." I can't see my group's faces but I know that they are looking at me like I am insane. My dad lights a candle and all of them except John looks at me like I am crazy.

"Ok, so I just got a call from Austin and things sound bad. My dad, John, Tom and I are going to get my cousin." This erupts the group, and almost wakes up the baby. Trinity says what Emily is about to say.

"Nope, Felix you are not going without me."

"Trinity, this is not up for argument. None of it is. You and Emily are staying because if you haven't noticed there is a baby in the group. Plus, we all know the way there, plus we will be fine. It is only a seven-hour drive." My dad pipes up, after that.

"It is six hours."

"No it is seven because of all the cars that are between us and our destination. Plus, we will be using back roads and not the highways." All of them look at me and I know that they will go along. The one who breaks the unbearable silence is John.

"Don't you think it is a little convenient that the power and the phone lines went down just when Austin was getting attacked? Plus, they went down at the same time." I just look at him with a smile.

"No, I mean it has been a week since the whole world was literally eaten by the undead."

"Don't you think that the power should have gone off before a week?" I have to bight my lip to keep from laughing.

"This is not a zombie book; this is real life." I look around and see the whole room biting on their lip.

"Dad, turn out the candle, we are going to sleep. I know we are all going to need it."

"Felix, I think you might need a few minutes with Trinity so I will let you turn out the candle." Everybody walks away except for Trinity.

"Felix, if you get hurt out there then I don't know what I would do."

"Trinity, have I ever let you down?"

"No." I walk up and give her a hug.

"Trinity, you know that I would do anything for you, but I have to do this. You know that if it was your cousin that you were close with, you would go. You know you would do it for me. You know I would do it for you. So just trust me and stay here. For me." She doesn't cry, all she does is hug me and I hug her back. I don't know why she doesn't cry, in matter of fact, I haven't seen her cry since the dead started rising.

"Trin, why haven't you cried since the world ended? I didn't even see you cry when we went to your house and your parents weren't there." She pushes away from me and looks me straight in the eyes.

"Felix, I didn't cry when I was stuck in a car with a group of zombies around me. I didn't cry when my parents and sister weren't in the house and I am not crying now. The only reason I didn't cry is because I am not a princess that needs a prince to save her. The events of the last week haven't caught up with me. I know I will cry when they do catch up with me, but that day is not today." She pauses and I can see that even now she isn't going to cry.

"Felix, you are the only thing I have left that I love. I love you, Felix Blank, and I know you love me. I know you don't want to lose me. I don't want to lose you. I know you think we are prepared for this but we aren't. We are just two teenagers that really don't want to lose each other." In the flickering candle light Trinity looks so beautiful. I start to talk.

"You know I still think of the first time I saw you. Do you remember the first time? You were walking down my street, and you were hanging out with Emily. You looked over at me and you saw me staring, well not staring, but taking a picture." She smiles, and almost laughs.

"Felix, I will never forget the day I met you."

"Trin, we should probably get to bed." She nods and I take her hand. We walk to the bedrooms. Before we got out of the kitchen, I blow out the candle and feel Trinity's hand tighten around mine. I go to bed smiling.

"Alright guys get your weapons and only pack a little food. Oh and don't forget the cd's." Tom and my dad look at me like I am crazy. John just looks like this is another day. My dad was always one to get up early, but not today.

"Come on Felix, we can go in an hour." I look at John, and he is smiling.

"Guys, get your butts up and get dressed. We need to go now. It is an hour before sun up and we need to get going. You can sleep in the car." They all moan and groggily get up. John is already dressed. I walk out of the room and go into the kitchen. I wait for them to get here and they come one at a time.

I have my knife, my dad has his rifle that he has always had, and John has that pistol that he picked up on the highway, and Tom has the bat.

"So, are we all ready? Do we have the cds?" Tom holds up a cd catalogue. I nod and toss my dad the keys.

"You will be driving to and from." He nods and I look at all of them.

"This will be a seven-hour trip tops. I left a note on the table so the rest of the group will know we left. They probably won't need it though." I take a deep breath and look them and then the door. I put my ear to it and hear slow moans. I put one hand on my knife and one hand on the doorknob.

Before I turn the knob, I look back and nod. They all nod back. I turn the knob. The dawn sky has always been one of the most beautiful things. Even with the dead rising it still is. I can't look at the sky right now; all I can look at is the monster at the door.

My step-mom used to know the guy at the door. He was a pretty nice, decent man. All of that is gone now. All that's left is the body, not the mind. I drop kick the zombie and it falls back and crashes down on the porch.

I don't even need my knife, I slam the heel of my foot, into the forehead of the monster. I keep ramming my heel, till John pulls me back.

"Felix, it's dead. We need to go." I look at him, and then to my foot, the blood stained sheet and my running shoes.

"I'm sorry, I don't know what happened." They all just look at me and I start walking to the car. I open the passenger's side and sit down. The rest come right after, and my dad turns on the engine, and we glide out of the neighborhood, and on to the highway. The car weaves its way through the abandoned cars.

I set my head on the window and look out. Mindless monsters notice the car for the first time and shambling to the car, then getting bored and going away. I look up at the sky, and watch the black melt away to become a luminescent pink, then orange, then blue. I close my eyes and drift off into a sleep.

I start to dream about Trinity; about the first time I saw her; the way the sun warmed her eyes and how the sun reflected in her brown hair. The first time she looked at me I was taking a picture. She thought that I was stalking her. The second word she said to me was off. I feel her shaking me and calling my name. I open my eyes to see my dad shaking me.

"Felix, wake up, we are going to stop." I sit up and wipe my eyes.

"What, where are we?" I look at my dad, and he is focusing on the road.

"We are just outside of New Orleans. That means you have been asleep for about thirty minutes."

"Why do we need to stop then, if…" I look around at all the people in the car dumfounded.

"We, forgot to check the gas before we started the road trip didn't we?" My dad nods.

"Well, I guess this is my fault. Wait, why did we go through New Orleans, you know that the city will be filled with zombies, as well as robbers."

"I don't know any other way to get to Houston. While we are at the gas station, we can get a map or something." I nod, and look at the back seats, then back at my dad.

"Wait the power is out, how are we going to pump the gas?"

"I guess siphon it from cars already there." I nod and look back out at the sky. The pink and orange have now turned into a deep vibrant blue. I always love to just look at the sky, while listening to music, especially with Trinity.

"So how much longer to the…" Tom doesn't even get to finish the sentence, when we see the cars on the highway.

"Dad, did you take the highway?" My dad stops the car, and looks at all of us.

"I did, I forgot." All I can do is stare at the massive pile up of the abandoned cars.

"It has only been a week. A week. How could it have gotten, this bad?" I look at my dad; he doesn't know about how much a germ can spread. How much a little disease could cripple and destroy everything that we have ever built.

"Dad, the disease must have spread faster than we thought. We couldn't have known." Billy says what we are all thinking.

"We can't go back. We don't have enough gas. We are going to have to walk." We all look at each other, then the massive ocean of cars. I try to lighten things up.

"What do you do with a dog from Endor? You take it for a Ewok." They all just look at me and my dad turns off the car.

"I will just shut up now." We all get out of the car, and put on our back packs we took when we left John's house, and we start the five mile trip from here to the nearest gas station to hotwire and steal a car.

"Guys, I think we can safely say that this is the best road trip we have ever been one. They just ignore me and walk away. I go after them, with one hand on the hilt of my knife, and twirling a coin Trinity gave me for my birthday.

"Every little thing will be alright." I repeat that over and over in my head to reassure myself. I look over to see Tom, and I walk right next to him.

"So how has your day been?"

"Oh fine, just working on my mile time." A smile spreads over both our faces.

"Yeah, me to. Don't worry we only have like four more miles to go, then we should be at my cousin's house and back by Monday."

"But, it is Sunday Felix."

"Exactly." I hear a loud moan, and I look over to the others, and we stop.

"You all heard that right?" They all nod, and we hear somebody fall. We all look to the back of us. A group of zombies had come out the side of the highway and followed us.

"Guys, we might just need to be quieter. Just a smidge really." We continue walking, and looking at the cars to the left and right of us. You can tell a lot about a person by their car. If the car is dirty, then they are a dirty person, or they have kids. If the car is clean, then they don't have kids, or they are really uptight about their cars.

I always liked looking at vintage cars. My favorite car in the whole world is the 1967 Chevrolet Impala. That is also the car that the main characters of one of my favorite TV shows drive. They are probably dead now, or they could be surviving with the cast of a popular zombie TV show. Who knows anymore? When the world ends you don't think about what happened to your favorite TV show actors, you think about your family or just you.

I was so lucky to have the girl I love be in my classroom when the dead started biting. Gosh, I love her. She is just like no others, cute, smart, funny, and she tolerates me. I start to think about how lucky I have been during the end of days. I mean one of my parents is still alive. So many others had to watch their parents die, or they killed them.

I look behind us and see the monsters still following us. More have joined them. The constant moan, and the stench of the first phase of decaying is all that fills the air, besides us breathing hard.

"How many miles have we walked?" I look at Tom.

"I really don't know, but this was a bad idea. We should have told them to come to us."

"Yeah, we should have." A voice coming out of nowhere, it sounds like it is coming from a microphone. All of us stop, and look at each other.

"Who said that?" My dad takes his rifle off of his shoulder, and John clicks the safety off.

"I did." We look behind us, and see the zombies catching up.

"Where are you?" I take my knife out, and the sun shine glints off of the blade.

"Look in front of you." We look in front of us to finally hear a motorcycle. The sound of the engine is actually silent. I look at my dad.

"Aim the scope, see if you can see his face, or anything we could use in our advantage." He aims the sniper, and the cyclist sees the glint of the scope.

"Put the rifle down. You will get shot. We do not allow warning shots, uses too much ammo." I look at my dad, and he puts the rifle down.

"Guys, he has a helmet on with flames on the side. He also has a hatchet attached to the side." I look at him, then I look behind me. The zombies aren't there, they are on the ground, with a river of blood streaming out of the bullet holes.

"They are behind us." The motorcycle gets closer, as I tighten my grip on my knife. John, I right beside me.

"Keep the safety off, we might need it, but go for wounding shots. We don't know who, or what they want. They might have children."

"Felix, you know that we will have to kill people, you know this. I know this. We all know this." I look at him, and our eyes connect.

"I know this buddy, but I will not kill right now, not until I have to. I know I will have to, but I don't right now. I will not cross that line. I am only fifteen." He nods and puts the gun back in the holster, but does not click the safety on.

"Dad, put the rifle over your shoulder, do not put the safety on. If it does come down to shooting, go for wounding shots."

"Why am I taking orders from you?"

"Because, I know this, I prepared for this." He nods and puts the rifle on his shoulder. The cyclist finally gets to us. He takes off his helmet and he has a scar going down one side of his face and blonde hair. He is wearing a typical biker outfit, complete with the leather.

"Are you friendly, and how many of you are there?" The man looks at my dad.

"That is not the first question you ask a stranger." The way he smiles, sends chills down my back. He looks at each of us as if he is sizing us up for something. His eyes move over each one of us, and he looks at all of our weapons. He's seeing if we are a threat to him.

He reaches to the back of his waistband and pulls out a walkie-talkie.

"Get out of the woods, all they are is a bunch of kids and an old man." I glance over at my dad, and I see him tighten his grip on the strap of his rifle. I look behind me to see four people walking out of the woods. They have a semi-automatic rifle, with a suppressor attached to the muzzle.

"Do you four have a camp around here?" The man has intentions I can only guess. My dad answers.

"No, we are just going to our cousin's house. We talked to her on the phone last night from Kenner."

"What are you going to do once you get there?" My dad almost freezes when he hears that question.

"Go see if the family in Chicago is ok." The man seems to be buying it. I look back and the men with rifles are right behind us.

I look at the man, then the bike. Something seems odd especially about the hatchet strapped to his belt.

"Where did you get that hatchet from sir?" He smiles that ugly smile, and I have to bite my cheek so I don't make an expression.

"Found it on a dead girl in Houston."

"Did you say Houston?"

"Yes. There was this blonde couple to, real tragic. He had a short sword and the blonde girl had throwing knives." The blonde couple part hit me like a train.

"Are they really dead?"

"Yes…"

"LIAR!" The man's smile fades, and he reaches for the hatchet and I reach for my knife. John pulls out the pistol and my dad pulls the rifle. The glint of the metal bat makes me think we can win if it comes down to a fight.

"You kids really think you can win against four rifles?" I look at Tom and see the look in his eyes. He wants to do something. The sad little boy I saw when he found his little sister and mom dead in his house is gone and instead replaced with pure, white hot fury.

"Did you kill the girl and the blonde couple?" The man looks like he was just asked a dumb question.

"We didn't kill them, they were teenagers. The whole reason we found them, was because we were tracking a group that stole from us." I let some of my tension go.

"Where are they?" He lets some tension go too.

"About a mile down the road. We made them come with us." My dad just looks mad.

"Just let them go and we can walk our different ways and never see each other again." My dad has his finger on the trigger and I can see where he is aiming. He is aiming for the thigh.

"Ok if that's all you want. All we are going to need is just your weapons."

"Yeah that's not gonna happen." The anger in my dad's voice grows with every word.

"Well, then you don't have a..." He doesn't finish the sentence. A crack goes off and the sound of a man falling on the ground fills the air. The men with the silenced rifles look at their leader and I can feel the cold metal of the suppressor on the back of my head. The leader is clutching a wound to his thigh. My dad walks to the bleeding man and takes him by the collar of the shirt and cold metal leaves the back of my head to aim at my dad.

"Tell me where my little niece is now or I will not hesitate to get that little teenager with the pistol to shoot you in the knee. In case you think I'm not telling the truth, you should know he is severely pissed. We don't know where his parents are. Oh and tell your guards to stand down." The man looks really, really mad, but he doesn't cry out in pain. All he does is call his men off.

"You've got some balls for an old man. Just know that you just made an enemy."

"Yeah I know that. Just remember I could have killed you." The man smiles, and laughs.

"Oh I know. Just remember I believe in an eye for an eye." Now it is my dad's turn to smile.

"I will be expecting it." My dad drops the man and picks up the hatchet.

"I will be taking this." My dad signals for us to follow him. We walk around the man and they watch as we walk away. My dad looks at us.

"Don't tell the girls." All of us smile at that, and we walk.

. . .

When Austin, Timmy, Megan, and Alex see us, they run to us. Austin and Megan have their weapons; Tommy looks like he was beaten by a pissed girlfriend.

"What happened to the little fart?" I can tell Austin is holding in a laugh. He answers anyway.

"Well your cousin has a little temper." Alex elbows him in the stomach, and looks at me.

"Actually, that little fart ran off after Austin punched him in the nose. I got sad, held hostage by a nice man, then got a weapon, which you are holding in your hand, then the fart came back with a gun, and killed my dad. So punched him in the nose again."

I start laughing, then I stop when I hear the moaning. I walk and hug Alex.

"Timmy should have known that you have a temper." I step away from Alex, and walk to Timmy. I whisper in his ear.

"You know I am all about second chances. So I will let you slide this time. But if you ever do that again I will give you two days' worth of food and drop you in the middle of nowhere." I look him in the eyes. "You better understand me." He nods.

"Ok let's go. We have about two hours to go till we get to the car." They all nod, and we start to walk back.

"So Austin, do you want to hear a Star Wars joke?"

"Is it the Ewok dog joke?" I look at him and just look away.

"No……" Austin laughs, and we walk. We walk for about another twenty minutes and we pass the spot where we met our first enemy. The bike is gone so is the wounded man. A blood trail is leading the way we first came. Megan says what Austin is thinking.

"So I assume you shot the man in the thigh."

"My dad did." She nods and looks away. Moans fill the air, so does the smell of the dead. We all look at each other and start to walk faster. John starts to make a joke.

"You know New Orleans kind of went to hell." I immediately realize what he is about to say, and I finish the joke.

"Yep, and we are on a highway. I guess you can say we are on the highway to hell."

We all start to walk a little faster. The moans get louder and the smell gets stronger. My dad has his rifle out and John has his pistol out. The more we walk the louder the moans get.

We finally see what we are hearing. A group of about twenty zombies walking towards us. I look at my group and motion to the woods surrounding the highway. I start to run and they follow, so do the zombies. While running I start to make a plan.

I have always done this. I have three functions, fight, flight, and get majorly screwed. The only way I get out of these situations is that I salute my solution.

"Remember when we got chased by those girls John?" He laughs as he runs.

"Yes, and I still remember why they chased us. But they were really cute."

"You have a girlfriend."

"So do you."

"Doesn't mean I can't think about the girls that I have ticked off in the past." I laugh and continue running. I motion for them to stop and all I hear is the heavy breathing. I look to the group.

"Remind me when we get back to start a mile running session." I walk to the edge of the woods and look to the edge of the car ocean. My hopes plummet to my shoes. The car we came here is gone. All we have is what we are carrying.

"Dad, did you leave the keys in the car? Did you forget the map in the car?" He searches through his pockets and his back pack.

"Yes, at the time I did not know we were going to meet Bike Man." I step out of the woods and into the middle of the highway, the rest follow.

"Ok, guys does anyone know how to hotwire a car?"

"Felix, I know how to." We all look at my dad, and stare at him.

"What? I am more than just a pretty face."

"Alright Dad, just pick out a car that we can get to and..." The moaning starts again and we all look to the woods. More zombies joined the group, which means we are even more royally screwed.

"John, Dad, kill as many as you can. The rest of us, will kill what you don't." They nod and start to aim. John takes the first shot; it goes directly into a zombie's head. Blood splatters as my dad takes the second shot. I knew that the rifle my dad is holding only has five shots total, and the pistol John is shooting has ten. But since my dad shot the Bike Man, he has four.

The gunfire continues as more and more zombies hit the ground. The last shot fills the air like cannon. I look at the remaining zombies. Eleven zombies are on the ground dead. I grip my knife even harder. I look at the rest of the group. Megan with her throwing knives, Austin with his short sword, Tom with his bat, and Alex with her hatchet.

"Tonight we dine in hell."

"Not the time for movie references Felix." I smile, and look at Tom.

"There is always a time for that." My dad and John get behind us with Timmy. The rest of us rush forward. I slam into the nearest zombie. It topples to the ground and I stab it through the eye. A volcano of blood splatters my blade. One down, don't know how many to go.

Out the corner of my eye I see Austin hacking and slashing and Megan making pin-point accuracy with her throwing knives. I put two hands around my knife and drive it into another zombie's eye. As it falls backwards my knife slides out of its eye.

I shake the knife and drops of blood rain on the ground. There are a few zombies left. I see Alex destroy a skull with her hammer. Tom smashes another one. A zombie is behind Alex, before it can bite into her, Austin impales the short sword through the head. It falls down as Alex turns around and thanks Austin. We all breathe hard.

I turn around to see Timmy fighting off a zombie with his bare hands. He is actually winning. He sweeps the knee and the demon wobbles then cascades to the concrete. Timmy picks up a rock the size of his head and bludgeons the skull of the hungry monster.

The inky red liquid bathes the ground. It geysers up on Timmy. He keeps hammering the dead monster until the head looks like a smashed pumpkin.

I look around and I see the whole group staring at him. I can see that they have gained a little respect for the boy who abandoned my cousin. I know I do. He stands up and drops the rock to the ground and looks at us staring at him. Timmy doesn't do anything. He just stares back at us. After, a few moments of uneasy silence, Timmy starts to talk.

"Let's go. I am sick and tired of being out here." We all nod and my dad goes to hotwire a car. Megan goes to collect her throwing knifes. Austin and Alex go to find a cloth to clean their blades with.

I do the same. I look through the car windows to see if they have any cloth. Luckily one does. I smash the window and unlock the door and see the keys in the ignition.

I look in the back seat and find the bandanna I saw. I take it and wipe the blood off my knife. When the knife is clean enough I sheathe it, and put the bandana in my back pack.

I make my way back to the rest of the group and see my dad just finished hotwiring a car. I get in the back seat and the rest file in. We don't talk the whole way. All we do is just look out the window and watch the sky fly by like a movie.

CHAPTER 6

FELIX

When you get in a hijacked car and ride through a city filled with dead people you realize how good society was. You also realize that taking out the garbage is a lot better than hoping you don't die. You also start to realize that there is probably a cure somewhere or there might not be. Most likely not. But one thing eats at you more than the zombies, is that you should have told somebody your feelings for them.

The person I should have told my feelings to was a girl I liked in eighth grade. She was pretty and she was on the volley ball team. She had long brown hair that flowed like melted chocolate, and her name was Kody. The whole reason I didn't ask her out or anything was because she got swept up in popularity.

The only reason I liked her (besides how cute she was) was that she was really smart. By the time we reached ninth grade, she was the most popular girl in school. She didn't talk to me or anyone she used to hang out with in middle school. I guess people change. I just hope I don't run into her. Last time I saw her, was at the end of our freshman year before she went to a private school. The last words I said to her were, "Hope you have a good life."

This was all before I met Trinity. If she turns up, I am so screwed. By the time we get back to John's house it is about two o'clock. Before we get out of the car we look around to make sure there are no zombies. When we make sure there are none, we get out and walk to the porch. Trinity opens the door before all of us are on the porch. She springs at me and almost breaks my back with her hug.

"Don't ever leave again without me knowing."

"I left you a note." She looks like she is about to kill me.

"I got the note but if you would have died out there I would have killed John." She looks at John and smiles.

"Why do you always threaten to kill me, when Felix dies?" We all laugh and hear the sound of slow moaning so we go inside.

John goes to Emily and we all meet in the kitchen. My dad tells everybody what happened. Then Alex tells everybody what happened in Texas; about how she met Zed and how Timmy left her and then came back. After we let the events of today sink in, I look around the kitchen table.

"We need to take that school. We all need guns. All of us. There is no time to teach everyone how to shoot and we don't have the space for it here. We will teach everyone how to shoot once we take the school." Austin looks at me like, I know what I am doing.

"Felix, how much ammo do we have? I mean I know your dad and John used a whole magazine." I look at my dad and he goes to get the bag he took from our house.

"For the rifle I have thirty rounds. John's gun is a nine-millimeter, and I have about forty rounds for that. But we only have two guns." Everet's dad, Michael, pipes in.

"Guys, before we learn how to shoot I think we all need weapons." We all look at each other, and I look at Michael.

"He is right. The gun situation can be handled by the base and the melee weapons has an easy solution. But I know the whole town of Belle Chasse has probably thought of this." They all look at me as if I just dropped a cliff hanger.

"We have our own hardware store filled with everything we need, duct tape, hammers. I mean they even have a glass box full of little pocket knives." I look at Christian.

"Christian, doesn't your uncle work at the hardware store?" He nods.

"How well do you know the store?"

"Like the back of my hand. When I was little, I used to go to work with my uncle; when my mom and dad had to work on the weekends." I smile.

"This will work. I really don't know the store that well, so buddy you will lead us." Michael and my dad look offended. My dad speaks for Michael and himself.

"What about Michael, and me?"

"You are both fully grown men. Christian is a fifteen year-old boy who just happens to go into the store all his life. He knows the new layout. You two know the old lay out." Christian pipes in.

"He is right." My dad and Michael nod.

"So the plan is to take the school in about a week or two." I look around the room; they all stare at me.

"In order to actually achieve that goal we need to get weapons. So before we can actually take the school, we need to have everyone ready to go." Everet looks at me and I can tell he is about to ask a question.

"What do you mean by getting everyone ready to go?"

"I mean, we need to have everyone able to kill. We need people to actually go into the school and we need people to kill the ones on the outside of the school as well." I look at Malcobe holding Elliot.

"Malcobe, I think you need to stay out front, someone will stay with you." She looks at me, then at Elliot.

"We don't have enough adults for that. We only have four adults and thirteen or fourteen teenagers. We are also going to need more than one car." We all look at her and I start to talk.

"She's right. We have more than twenty people. All of us will have to go to the school but we can't take cars. We need to walk."

"Why can't we take cars?" We all look at Michael. John answers the question he just asked.

"The sound will draw the zombies, plus the road to the school is full of abandoned cars. We were lucky to find a car that could get us through the road." Michael nods. I nod and I start to talk.

"We will go to the hardware store tomorrow. I don't know if we all should go or not. I was thinking I could leave that decision up to all of you." They nod.

"So, are we all going?" Malcobe looks at me.

"I can't go." I nod.

"Alright. I think that some of us will stay here. The people who already have a weapon will stay but I will be going because I need to see something while we are out there." They all nod and I look at Christian.

"Christian, you will take the ones who don't have the weapons. Michael and my dad are going to be with you. John and I will go to check what I need to check." John looks at me.

"What do you need to check?"

"I need to check a house by the store." They nod and my dad looks at me.

"Are you sure you can handle that?"

"Yeah, it will be fine." He nods.

"Ok everyone, let's get some rest. Timmy, you should fit into some of my clothes." Timmy nods.

"I will show you to where my stuff is and then we should all get some rest." He nods and I walk out of the kitchen, Timmy follows me. I show Timmy where my clothes are.

"Pick anything." He nods and I walk out of the room. I go to the living room, and plop down onto the couch and fall asleep. Images of before the end of the world flash in my dream.

The thing I see the most are faces of my friends and family. Some smiling, some not. I see the last time I saw my step-mom. How I said I loved her before I went to school on that Monday morning. She said it back and I left to catch the bus.

The scene changes and I see the first time I saw Trinity crying. Her grandmother died while we were at an end of the year dance for the eighth graders. She looked at her phone right after we slow danced. That was the first time I had to comfort her. It was also the first time I kissed her. I kissed her behind the gym.

It was amazing. It was also my first kiss. I have never felt that way before. Then the scene changes and I see the first time I met John. I met him in the first grade. We met waiting for to go into the principal's office. There was this kid who was making this other kid cry and I tackled him. John saw this and joined in. The scene changes again. This time it isn't a memory. It is a nightmare.

I just stand in the middle of school courtyard seeing Alex being eaten by a zombie. It rips strips of flesh off the bone. I am frozen to the spot; forced to watch a monster feast on my cousin. Her face is the worst thing about the scene. Her eyes are wide in terror and her mouth is the form of a scream and tears mix with the blood. Before the scene is painted by a black abyss, she says two words. Two words that will haunt me forever. "Help Me."

. . .

I jolt up on the couch and look around. I run my hand through my hair and get off the couch. I stand up and notice that there is no sun shining through the windows. It must still be night time. I walk to the bathroom. I walk past the rooms filled with sleeping people trying to survive in a world that now wants all of us dead.

I get to the bathroom and go to turn on the light. The switch doesn't work and I remember that the electricity is off. I walk into the bathroom in total darkness. I try my best not to stub my toe on the toilet but I know I will. Once I find the toilet, I relieve myself and replay the nightmare over and over in my head.

I finish and head back to the couch but before I go to the couch I open the door to the room where the girls are sleeping and look for Alex. She is sleeping next to Megan. I close the door and head for the couch. I walk into the living room, and stretch out on the couch.

I try to go to sleep but I can't. Instead of sleeping I just stare at the ceiling. I think about fun times I had with my friends.

I think about the time I went to a festival my town had. This was before I met Trinity and it was more embarrassing than funny from my perspective. John and I decided to go and ride a ride. The ride was called The Flyer. You lay flat on your stomach and you are spun around. We rode it a total of six times. Long story short, we threw up. John threw up on the ride and I threw up on my pants. I don't regret a single moment of it.

I laugh to myself and I close my eyes. This time I am able to go to sleep. This time I don't have a nightmare. I just replay the festival/throw up memory. It feels like I am asleep for five minutes when I open my eyes to see Trinity and Emily standing in front of me. I sit up.

"So, are we all ready to go? I know I am." They look at me then they look back at each other. I notice something is wrong.

"What's wrong?" Trinity opens her mouth to speak but then closes it. Emily speaks for her.

"Felix, Timmy left last night." I stand up and look at them.

"What do you mean Timmy left last night?"

"What we mean is that Timmy is gone. We don't know where he went but what we do know is that he took nothing." I start to rub my thigh.

"We don't need him anyways. What we need is to go to the hardware store and get everyone ready for taking the school." They nod and walk to the room where the girls are. Alex walks into the living room and she has a blank face.

I think about going to talk to her but then think she needs to be alone. So I just go to the room where the boys have their stuff. I open the door and head to my bag. I look for my belt but I feel it around my waist. I look around the room to see the guys who are going to the hardware getting ready.

"Ok, everyone going to the store, hurry up. We need to leave." They nod, and I walk out of the room and go to the girl's room. Before I open the door I knock.

"Does everyone have clothes on?" Megan answers me. "Yes." I turn the knob and open the door.

"Everyone that is going to the store get ready." I turn to Malcobe.

"Malcobe, I think you should come with us. Just leave Elliot here with the people that have weapons." She nods and I walk out. I walk into the living room and see that Alex isn't at the kitchen table anymore. She is on the couch where I was.

"Ok Alex, we are about to leave so I will see you in a few hours." She nods and I go to the kitchen table to wait for all the people going to the store. The people that are going to the store are; Christian, my dad, Michael, myself, John, Emily, Trinity, Everet, Martini, and Malcobe. It takes a total of twenty minutes for all of them to get ready. When they get here I tell them the plan.

"Guys, when we get to the store, just follow Christian and don't leave the store till John and I get back." They nod, and we go to the front door. Before, we leave my dad checks to make sure that his rifle is fully loaded. John checks his pistol one more time. We all file out of the house and onto the street.

I am in the front with Christian and my dad. We jog down the street and the stench of dead people is stronger than it was when we first came. When we get to the highway we hear the familiar moan. It sounds distant but the moan gets stronger with every step. As we jog down the street, we see some zombies just walking but they don't notice us.

After five minutes we make it to the store and we stop. The windows of the store are intact, not even a crack. The glass door is also intact. I look at the group.

"Christian, is there a back door?"

"Yes, there is." I nod and take my knife out of it's sheathe.

"Take them around back. John and I will go do what I need to do." He nods and starts to walk to the back of the store while John and I start to jog to the street.

"Felix, where are we going?" I look at him and then back at the street that leads off the highway and into a neighborhood.

"John we are going to check something. What we need to check is a house that I know has a lot of guns which we need." He nods.

"How do you know that this house has a lot of guns?"

"My step-mom used to be friends with him."

"How do you know that they are not alive?"

"I don't." John smiles.

"I always love what happens next when you say those words."

"What do you mean John?"

"Whenever you say I don't know or I don't, something always happens."

"Nothing happens when I say those words."

John looks at me like I am stupid.

"Do you not remember, when you went to go talk the girl you had a crush on before Trinity? It took you a whole semester for her to notice you." I think about that for a second.

"Yeah, that semester was the worst I have ever had."

"Yeah, it was. You were so mad that she didn't notice you." We laugh about that and jog the rest of the way in silence. It takes us three minutes to get to the house. We stop in front of the house, and breathe for a few minutes. The house looks to be about twenty years old but it has a charm to it.

"Let's do this." I say that as John clicks his gun out of the safety position. I tighten my grip on my knife as I walk to the door of the house. I grip the door knob and turn it. The door is unlocked I look at John and nod. He nods back. I open the door and John aims into the dark doorway.

John steps into the black void first. He has his finger on the trigger and I have my right hand on the handle of my knife. Before we walk deeper into the apartment, I close the door behind us.

I fish a little keychain flashlight out of my pocket. I click it on and a small stream of light illuminates the darkness in front of us.

John starts walking and I go after him. A weird smell fills the air as we walk. I look to the right of me and notice that dried blood stained a wall. John keeps walking so do I. The small beam of light picks up a living room. I turn off the light as I see the windows lighten up the area. When we get into the room I almost drop my knife.

The man my step-mom once knew has a gun in his hand. The back of his head has an exit wound. I look at John and he looks pale. We move closer to the dead body and I notice a note. My heart almost stops when I read it.

"God forgive me for taking Jen's life. She didn't deserve what happened to her." I look over at John and I can see that he needs to puke.

"Let's just get this over with so we can go back. The smell is killing me." John nods. He picks up the gun that the man used to kill himself with. The gun is a small revolver. At max ammo it can hold six bullets. But there are only five bullets in it. John hands it to me.

"Take this. It won't be much but it will be enough for now." I nod and put my knife back into it's sheathe. I take the handle of the gun and cock it.

"Alright, we find what other guns or ammo we can find and find a backpack or something." John nods, and we go into the kitchen. Nothing. I go to the sink and turn on the faucet, nothing comes out.

"Looks like they turned off the water." I look at John.

"Where are we gonna pee now?"

"We will figure that out when the time comes." He laughs and we go through the door at the back of the kitchen. It leads to a hallway. The hallway must lead to the bedroom or something. There are still windows so I don't use the keychain flashlight.

We walk down the hallway and at the end of it, is a door. John knocks on it to make sure nothing is in it. After a few seconds he opens the door. The only thing that comes out of the room is the smell of death. We walk in the room and see a crib. Blood coats the sheets of the crib like paint. What we see on the other side of the room is forever seared in my brain like a brand. We see a dead zombie with dried blood on its hands and a half-eaten body of a toddler. John and I look at each other.

"Wrong room." John looks worse than he did before. We walk out of the room, and back down the hallway to the living room then. Then we walk down the hallway that leads to the front door to find the master bedroom. With luck and a keychain flashlight we find the master bed room. We don't have to knock on the door this time. We now the only thing in this house is death.

This time I am in the lead. I open the door to see a room with one window. The window has no curtains and the bed is stained with blood. We see a cabinet on the other side of the room. It is wide open. Inside of the cabinet are guns and boxes of ammo.

There are rifles, pistols and shotguns. A collector's dream cabinet. I look at John, he is a mix between wanting to puke, and wanting to cry.

"This guy was a collector. My dad had a cabinet like this."

"Why didn't we find any guns in your house then?" John looks at me and I can see anger start to fill his eyes.

"My dad keeps his collection in a storage container that he probably emptied when he decided not to wait for his only child."

"John calm down." John tenses up and then relaxes.

"Sorry." I don't respond to that. All I do is start looking for a bag or something to put all the guns in. I find one next to the cabinet. John and I start to load up the boxes of ammo, the guns, and the magazines for the guns. It takes us about thirty minutes to get everything in the bag. I look at John and he looks dazed and distracted.

"Who is going to carry this? We have at least thirty guns." John snaps out of his day dream and looks at me.

"I guess I will." He picks up the bag of guns, and we start to walk out of the room. We walk down the hallway to the front door and we walk out the house. I take a big breath.

"You know John, fresh air has never smelled so good."

"Yeah." John sounds distant.

"What's wrong buddy?" He looks at me, and sighs.

"I started to think about what happened to my mom and dad. Just imagining what happened to them makes me want to cry but I know I can't cry." I study his face before I say anything. I have seen the look on his face before. I've seen it in the mirror and on Alex's face this morning when she was sitting on the couch.

"John, you can cry, you know you can, but you don't want to. I know what it feels like. I talked to Trinity about this before." I stop talking to look back at the house. The image of the half-eaten baby jumps into my head.

"All of us will cry. We don't know when or what will happen to make us cry. But we all know that it will happen. All we can do is hope that when the time comes, all of our loved ones are safe." He nods and we start to walk back to the store silent. It takes us about ten minutes to get back to the hardware store.

When we get back to the store John and I look at each other and we walk to the back door. The door is left wide open. John smiles like he just thought of a joke.

"You know what they say, love is an open door." I look at John and I can't help but smile.

"Why do we have to bring up that movie in the middle of the zombie apocalypse?"

"So what you're saying is that I need to let it go."

"John, shut up." We laugh as we walk through the door way except this time I close the door. The moment I close the door, darkness washes over us. Without even thinking about it I reach into my pocket and pull out the keychain flashlight.

The beam breaks through the darkness like a bullet through a glass sheet. A small narrow beam pulses its way through the inky sheet in front of us. We both walk through the back way until we find a door that leads us into the big room where the costumers shop.

"Do you think they call the room where you buy stuff, the show room John?" He looks at me with a smile.

"I don't know but that's what I am going to call it." We laugh as we enter the room. I turn off the light and smile. I haven't felt this good since the end of the world started. All I know is that this isn't going to last. The safer people feel, the faster they let their guard down. When you let your guard down something sneaks past you, and when something sneaks past you, someone dies.

I keep walking with a hand on my knife. I will not let my guard down. I will not let someone die. We get to the tool section to see the rest of the group messing with the tools. I see Malcobe has a crowbar and Everet has a hammer. I look over at Everet.

"How's life?" Everet smiles.

"Oh its fine." We laugh as John asks a question. "So why was the back door open?" Everet's dad answers.

"Because we needed light to find the door into the building."

"Don't you think that zombies or people would have walked through the open door?" Michael looks away then back at John.

"All I am saying is that people never go for the back door." I nod.

"Now all you have to hurry up and pick your weapons. John and I will get batteries and other essentials." My dad stops me from going by asking me a question. "What is in the duffle bag?"

"Guns and ammo." They whole group looks at us.

"I think you should leave that with us." I nod and John takes the bag off and gives it to my dad. When we walk off I hear the sound of him unzipping the bags.

"They are so going to question us when we get back." I look at John and he nods. I laugh and we walk to the flashlight aisle. The aisle is filled with every type of flashlight imaginable. They even have a flashlight in the shape of a bat. John and I look at each other.

"Which ones do we need?" I look at John as I pick up the flashlight bat thing.

"I think we need this one. I mean it is a bat and a light. What other protection do we need now that we have this?" He laughs at my sarcasm.

"Ok, so just grab whatever you think we need." Before he walks down the aisle, he turns to me.

"Take the bat light thing. I think it will be funny to use." I laugh while I pick up as many flashlights and batteries I can hold. After about five minutes, the rest of the group walks up to us. My dad is the first to speak.

"Where did you get all these guns?"

"Remember that Frank guy that Janet used to talk to?"

"Yes."

"He was a gun collector. He died. John and I saw what happened to him. I don't think I have to finish that statement." My dad rubs his thigh. I get the rubbing my thigh from my dad.

"No, you don't." I change the subject after that.

"So, can we leave now?" He nods his head and I call John back. We head to the back door before we leave the store. I look at the newly armed group in front of me.

"Now that everyone is armed, we will wait a week and then take the school." I see heads nodding as I turn to open the back door. I hear moaning coming from the other side. I look back.

"Change of plans. We will be going out of the front." They all nod as we head through the show room. We move silently, as possible. We finally make it to the automated front doors and I start to rub my thigh.

"This really escalated quickly huh." I try to bring some humor to the situation but it doesn't work. We make it to the front door and we all realize that the door doesn't open. I look around at all the people behind me. They stare at me like I don't have an idea.

"Can any of you hand me something hard?" Malcobe hands me her crowbar.

"Yeah, uh why did you nee…" The sound of shattering glass cuts her off. A million tiny diamonds litter the ground. I look back at the group. They are all in shock. They all look at me like I need a therapist. My dad is the first one to break the silence.

"You can't just go around and shatter a glass door." Before I walk through the door I turn around and look at my dad.

"Yeah, but what I just did was a shattering experience." This time its John's turn to break the silence.

"You also can't just go around making bad puns." I ignore him as I walk out of the store. They follow as I pick up the crowbar. I walk to Malcobe and hand her the crowbar. She has a smile on her face as I hand her the weapon. I start to talk to her as we walk across the parking lot.

"Why do you have a smile on your face?"

"Because I thought that pun that you said was pretty funny." I smile at that.

"Thank you." My smile falls flat as I ask her something.

"Do you think that the school is the right place? Do you think that I am the right one to call the shots here?" She goes silent for a minute before answering my question.

"Felix, I have known you for about two years and I was only your teacher but I've seen how you reacted to kids that did not like you. You acted like a leader but you are only fifteen. Some of the people who rely on you are a lot older than you. They also don't know how to react in situations that we have been faced with. They also don't know about how to survive." I look at her and she doesn't have a smile either.

"I can do this now, but I will need help later."

"We all do." She leaves me with that as she walks off. I just repeat what she said in my head and think about it the whole way back to the house. I pull that thought down when I see the house. I just replace the bad things with good things. When I push the image of the baby down, I realize that in order to survive you have to push bad things down. If you dwell on the bad things, you will die.

. . .

"Are we all ready? I mean before we actually do, this I want to make sure that we don't have any problems." I look around the table one last time. This will be the last time any of us will talk around this table. None of them say anything, nor do any of them look sad about this.

"Why are none of you sad about this? I mean we are about to kill our past peers and teachers. I mean we might not know most of them but they were people." John has to hide his smile.

"Notice how you said were. Were is the key word in that sentence." I just look at John like he is crazier than he already is.

"You are as cold as ice." He smiles.

"Yes, I am also ready to sacrifice." That makes the rest of us smile.

"Ok, so the bags are packed and we are ready to go, then let's go." We all pick up a bag or two and we head to the door. I am at the back of the group, John in front of me. I look and see John looking around his house one last time.

"So, I guess this is good bye, huh Felix?" I look at him; he looks the same as I did when I was in my house. He looks the way we all looked in our house.

"Don't worry, maybe some other group will make use of this place." He smiles at that. Before we leave, he says one last thing.

"Maybe that group will be my mom and dad, maybe they will come back." I look back at him and his smile is gone. So is mine.

"Yeah, maybe." We walk out and we don't bother locking the door. As we walk I think about all that happened these past two week. All of the demons I killed, all the things I said. The one thing that stands out of all that happened this week is that man my dad shot. He is probably still out there, probably holding a grudge. The worst part of thinking about that is knowing we left the keys in the car. How could we be so reckless?

A low moan shakes me out of my day dream. I look around and I reach for my knife and I get everyone's attention.

"Guys did you hear that?" They all nod.

"We just need to be a little quieter. I mean we all have guns but I don't want to have to use them. Mainly because not all of us are trained to use them." They nod and keep walking. As they do, I get lost in thought again. I think about what is going to happen in a day or two. I think about the school and how John and I saw that big group of zombies by the library.

But a question keeps eating at me. It's been eating at me since we decided to take the school. Am I going to be able to kill the zombified remains of my teachers and peers? I keep flipping the question like a coin in my head. As we walk, none of us make any noise. All of us know the risk of making a noise. None of us want to die on these streets, doomed to an eternity of walking the Earth searching for human flesh to feed the undying hunger.

. . .

It takes us almost half a day to make it to Everet's house. We stop there to rest. Still none of us talk. We are all too lost in exhaustion to talk to each other. We stay at the house for about an hour. The hour is full of rest and silence. We all switch bags, to make sure none of us get too tired. I am carrying the bag of food. The plan now is not to stop till we get to the school. The school is about seven miles from the military base, which Everet's house is in front of.

Lucky for us, people live by the school so we can sleep there for tonight and plan how we are going to take the school. We don't know how many zombies are in the school or if the school is already occupied, but what we do know is that either way, we will get into that school.

We also got lucky. We got lucky by that people will take us in if someone is already in the school. They'll take us in because it has only been two weeks and that means that people aren't too screwed up to not let us in. That also means that we aren't too screwed up to attack the group if they don't let us in.

. . .

While walking through an endless wave of cars never to be driven again it makes you think of what you did before the end of the world. The one thing that happened to me before the dead started rising, I think about is the day I met Trinity. When I first saw her I was taking a picture to test my new camera I got for my birthday and she walked into the frame.

The first time I talked to her was the first time I actually used a cheesy pick-up line. I smile to myself as I think about how stupid that sentence was. The line went something like this, "Do you have a map? Because I just keep getting lost in your eyes." The look on her face when I told her that line was the funniest thing I have ever seen.

Dozens of loud moans shake me out of my thoughts. The whole group looks back and we see about twelve zombies shuffling towards us. I walk to the front of the group to get their attention.

"Ok so like we might have to take the zombies. There are more than ten of us and we all have weapons that we know how to use. Plus, we have guns with ammo." The whole group looks at me like I am bat crap crazy. I look past them to see how much time we have left to decide what to do.

"Ok, if you people don't want to fight then just give me another idea." I look at all of them and they just look back at me. I take my knife out of the sheathe, so does Austin and Megan and even Alex. Before the fight actually begins, I glance around. Everyone in the group is ready. They are still the same people I saw two weeks ago. Something hits me I knew all along. This won't last, these people will change I mean we might not show what has changed yet but we will. All of the survivors left in this damned world, will show how we deal with these things. That's the one thing we all have to look forward to other than death.

I tighten my grip on my knife so hard my knuckles turn white. No matter how many zombies I have to kill, I will never get used to fighting to live. The first zombie approaches and Alex takes it out. The zombie is shorter than Alex so all she has to do is chop. Instead of chopping she thrusts the hammer side of the hatchet down. Blood flies and smears Alex with a thin layer of inky red blood.

The rest of the zombies shuffle toward us. One down, eleven to go. The next one is taken out by a gun. I look at John.

"Good shot." He nods and lines up another shot. I stand there and wait for a zombie. There is no sense in running to a group of zombies when I have a group of people. Plus, I still have that gun that John gave me. I pull out the gun and cock it.

All I can think about is the basic technique I was taught when I first held a gun. Look and pull. I do just that and I hit what I am aiming for. I cock the gun again and do the same thing. I do the same thing till the bullets run out.

You can probably hear the fight about a mile away. My dad, John and I are shooting guns while the rest of the group waits for when we run out of ammo. This will probably be the same thing tomorrow, expect maybe the three of us won't shoot all of the zombies in one sitting.

When the last zombie drops, all of us breathe a sigh of relief. I look around to see Elliot on the verge of crying. She must have been scared by the unexpected loud sounds. I would have been, if I was a two year-old in this damned world.

After about three minutes of just standing there, we turn around and start walking to the school. None of us talk about what just happened, nor do any of us talk. Just like the last five miles all you hear is the baby and our shoes hitting the pavement.

The worst part about the end of the world is getting used to the silence. Just imagine, all the sounds you have gotten used to, like cars and planes, they all just stop one day. I couldn't imagine it till two weeks ago. It all seems like it happened so sudden. I mean all it took was one day, one day for everything to go dark. It took me a week to get used to it, even with a whole group of friends to talk to.

The other thing that gets me in this new world is how some of the people in this group will die, and I will have to mourn them. The first time I had to mourn someone was when I was six. I wasn't really close with the person who died, but I knew I had to be sad, and I was sad. All I know is the first one to die won't be the last.

After about three hours of walking, we finally get to the school. The bad thing about that is it is swarming with zombies. You can smell them a mile away. When we finally get there, we all give a sigh of relief that we don't have to walk anymore. Before we can do anything about taking the school we need to rest and eat.

We turn around to look at the houses across the street from the school.

There are about six of them. The yards used to be well manicured but now they are decaying like everything else dead in this world. We choose the nicest house, which coincidentally doesn't have cars, which means, most likely there are no people in the house. Before we go into the house, I get in front of the group and scan the crowd.

"Today we have just walked fourteen miles within twelve hours. That is the most I have ever walked and that means tomorrow we clean out the school and finally get a permanent base of operations." I look at each person.

"For the rest of the day, we rest, because tomorrow we have to kill the reanimated corpses of our peers." They all look down at that last comment. I still look at them. I start to talk again.

"So, let's get going. The sun is starting to set and I really don't want to be out after dark in this part of town after sunset." They smile and we start to go into the house. The only thing I can think about while walking into the house is a question that I hate asking myself. Will anyone die tomorrow?

. . .

The morning of taking the school did not take us by surprise, we all know what we will be doing in about an hour. We all know that in about an hour we will be faced with a situation that no one should ever do; kill people they went to school with. The more I think about it the more I hate the idea. But the more I look out across the highway and I see the safety of that school makes me want to get it over with.

Before I can think anymore, John taps me on the shoulder, and hands me a gun and a holster.

"This is a Beretta 92, it is a semi-automatic, handgun that you will be using today in the school. It has a twelve bullet clip, which is currently full." I take the gun and look at him.

"Did you find a weapon besides the gun yet?" He smiles and looks at the knife on my belt.

"Yes, I found a hatchet in the shed." I smile and I stand up and walk with him to the kitchen. I look around the table to see the group looking as tired as I feel.

"Ok, so today is the day, the day when we take the school. I can tell we are mostly ready for this. Plus, we get a work out." They all smile after that.

"Not all of us will be going. I mean we have about over ten people. Plus, we have a baby and not all of us are fighters yet." I think over that last word, then I snap out of it.

"We will enter through the front office, then make our way through the halls and if there are too many we find the nearest room, and lock ourselves into it. Plus, I think we should take some extra ammo for incase we get trapped into a room." I stop to catch a breath and look around the kitchen.

"Now, I think Malcobe should stay here with Martini." Malcobe and Martini look at me, then they look at the baby in Malcobe's arms, Malcobe starts to speak.

"Look, before we go into the school guns a blazing, I think we should look around and try to find some walky-talkies." After she says that, she looks around the room, then they all look at me. Before I start talking John slips out of the room.

"Good idea, but I don't think we could find any walki…." Before I can finish, John walks back in the room with three walki-talkies.

"Ok, so I could only find three walki-talkies, so I think that Felix should carry one and the other two should stay here." I nod and John tosses me one.

"Thanks John." I turn to face the rest of the group.

"Ok go get ready, get ammo, guns, and enough weapons so we don't get killed in an hour." They all nod and walk out of the room. When they are all out of the room, I sit down in a chair and let out a sigh of relief. John walks back in the room with a back pack.

"Felix, why do you look so sad?"

"I don't know John. It may be that we could possibly lose someone when we go into that hell hole." John's face goes from happy to sad.

"Buddy, we will not lose anyone. We will kill our reanimated peers and we will make that school our home." I just look at him and smile.

"I bet no teenager has ever said, 'we will make that school our home'." He smiles after that.

"Well, we have been saying that for about two weeks." I laugh and stand up.

"John, I am going to go get ready for school." He nods and I walk to the bedroom with the gun in my hand. When I get there, I put on a pair of jeans, my favorite shirt and my shoes. Before, I walk out of the room, I strap on the gun and my knife. I breathe for a few seconds and then pray. "Please don't let anything happen to any of my friends and family out there in that school. Amen." After that, I step out into the living room where everyone is ready to go.

Before we actually go out the door of the house, I look at everyone who is going: Christian, John, my dad, Michael, Everet, Trinity, Tom, Alex, Megan, Austin, Billy, and Emily. I scan their faces and as I stand in front of the group, I think of something to say.

"Today, we are warriors and tomorrow we are survivors." They all stare at me as I turn around and clip the walky-talky to my belt. As we walk through the doorway, all I can do is hope that God heard my prayer.

CHAPTER 7
ALEX

The moment we step outside of the house. I see the school. The school that I have never set foot in, the school filled with monsters. Seeing the school reminds me of Timmy I don't know why he left the first time nor do I know why he left when we got to John's house.

All I know is I am pissed. The images of Timmy and me laughing and enjoying each other's company rage through my mind like a hurricane. The more I think of him the more rage fills me. I snap out of thinking about him when we get to the gate of the school. Felix starts talking.

"Ok, here is the plan, we enter through the front doors, look through each room and kill what's ever in the rooms and move on. We might have to go in groups of two in each room so we can do this faster. So I would buddy up if I were you." He stops talking and moves by John. Everet moves by me.

"So do you wanna be buddies?" I stare at him, like he is an idiot.

"This isn't a school field trip. But since Felix said we need to, I guess you can be my buddy." He smiles at that, as he tightens his grip on his hammer. I tighten my grip on my hatchet thing Zed gave me.

We walk across the front parking lot and up the steps to the front office. Before, we open the doors to go into the building, Felix talks again.

"I will take the principal." We all nod as we walk into the building. The moment we walk into the building I start to gag. The smell of rotten flesh and dead bodies fill the air like a strong perfume. We hear the first moan as the principal walks out of his office.

Felix moves into attack mode like in the movies. He jumps over the low desk and stabs the principal through the eye. Blood splatters the blade like a water balloon popping. Felix nods as he makes his way back to the front of the group. He signals us to move, so we do. It only takes us a few seconds to make our way to the first hallway, since the senior hallway is literally the first hallway you walk into. Felix stops us as he begins to talk.

"Ok, so you should have paired up. Each pair will take a room. Once you finish that room, go to the next until we are all done." We nod as we split up. I look to Everet.

"So which room do you want to go to? I really don't know my way around the school." He nods and points to the room at the end of the hall. I nod and take the lead. The room he pointed to reads 'Science Lab' on the door. I turn the nob and the door opens. We see three zombies lying on the floor in puddles of their own blood.

I take the first one. I lift my hatchet over my head and bring it down like a hammer. The blade connects with the skull as blood geysers the blade. I move to the next zombie, and do the same thing. I look over at Everet, and his face is long.

"Did you just kill one of your friends?" He nods.

"His name was Jeremy; I didn't really actually talk to him but seeing him soaking in his own blood as a reanimated corpse got to me." I nod as we leave the room.

The rest of the hall is empty, except for some eaten bodies. Every time we pass by an eaten body, I check to see if it is Timmy. I don't know why I do, but I do. I mean, after all he did to me, I shouldn't even be able to think about him, while smiling.

The more I think about him, the more I feel hatred. I feel white hot rage. The rage fills me like water. I can't release the rage until I see another monster that ruined my life. I am thrust out of my thoughts when the rest of the group finish their rooms. Felix starts to talk.

"Ok, this went well. I mean, no one got bit nor did we see any actual walking zombies. So on to the next hallway." He starts to walk to the next hallway as Everet starts to talk to me.

"So we did some good team work back there." I look at him without a smile.

"Are you hitting on me?" His face goes bright red like a cherry.

"Why, would I hit on you? Um.... No, I....."

"I don't know you but you sure are acting like an idiot." His smile fades.

"I really didn't hit on you." John over hears us and makes a joke.

"That's what a guy who hit on a girl would say." Everet's face goes even brighter.

"Look, all I was saying Alex, is that we did good work back there." A frown forms on my face.

"That's how my last boyfriend hit on me." Everet's smile fades completely as he walks to his father. Felix fills his spot.

"That was harsh older cousin. I mean you could have been just a little bit nicer." I look at him with a blank face.

"I really could have been a little nicer. Felix, you could be a little more helpful with Timmy baby cousin." I walk to the front, but I hear one last thing from Felix.

"She is a heartbreaker, dream maker, and a love taker." I feel so relieved when we reach the next hallway. I look back at Felix.

"What hallway are we in?"

"We are currently in the junior wing of the school. We just cleared out the sophomore wing." I nod, as, I walk to the nearest classroom. Everet is right behind me. I let Everet open the door as I stand behind him. The smell hits me before the door opens.

The familiar moans hit me after the smell. After Everet enters I follow him, as I tighten the grip on my weapon. The first zombie comes from behind me and grips my shoulder. I hit the jaw of the monster with my shoulder, I turn around and kick the monster to the wall. I slam the hammer part of the weapon down as blood smears the wall behind it. I stagger back, as I breathe hard,

Everet kills a zombie at the back of the classroom. Everet starts to breathe hard too. I turn around and look at him.

"When were you going to tell me that there was a zombie in front of the room?" He smiles.

"Maybe we should have better communication." I almost smile at that.

"Now that was flirting." He doesn't get embarrassed this time, he just goes with it. His smile turns sly.

"So, like do you want to go to another room?" I nod as we walk out of the room into another room. This time there are three zombies in the room. I recognize none of them but when I turn around to see Everet's face, I can tell he knew at least two of them. Everet goes in front of me and kicks one of the zombies in the stomach and hammers the other one in the eye with the nail puller part of the hammer.

I slam the hammer part of the hatchet on the skull of the third zombie. It slams into a desk when it falls. After it falls, Everet slams a foot on the monster's head. The head pops like a water balloon. Blood geysers on Everet's shoe and the floor.

"Nice team work partner." Everet's sly smile is still there.

"I'm not your partner. I am only in your survivor group." He smiles and shakes his shoe to get some of the blood off. I walk out of the classroom, leaving him behind.

"Well, I see that you're still little miss sunshine." I almost smile at that, as I turn around to see Felix. Everet walks out of the room.

"So, I can see that Evert got to play a little footsie with a zombie." I hide a smile after that. I turn around to see Everet walking up behind me along with the rest of the group.

"Ok, so guys we are going to the freshmen hall now." I nod and follow the rest of the group. When we get to the freshmen wing, Everet points to a room and I nod.

"Look Everet I think I will go in first this time." He nods and I open the door. Three students and a teacher.

"I will take one of the students and the teacher." Everet nods, as he jumps into action. I jump at the teacher first. I kick the teacher in the knee and I slam the hatchet in the skull of the zombie. The cut opens and blood flows like a river.

I try to pull the hatchet out but it won't budge. I let go of the handle as I hear a moan behind me. I look back to see the student fumbling through the maze of desks. I look around and run to the teacher's desk. I rummage through the drawers looking for something to fight with.

Nothing. I ball hands into fists. I ready myself to launch at the zombie. But, before I launch the zombie drops. Everet pulls his hammer out of the head of the zombie. Between heavy breaths, Everet starts to talk.

"So, I can see that you needed a little help." I smile for the first time in a week.

"My knight in shining armor." The sarcasm in my voice is unmistakable.

"I knew I could make you smile." The smile on Everet's face while he says, reminds me of Timmy. I walk to the dead teacher and I pull my hatchet out of the head of the zombie. I walk with Everet into another room. Before we enter the room, we see John and Felix enter another room.

Everet opens the door and I tighten my grip on the hatchet. There is only one zombie in this room. I let Everet take this one. The zombie collapses on the floor. He turns around and smiles at me.

"So, how did I make you smile at me? I mean your cousin has been trying to make you smile all week."

"I don't know why I smiled at you, maybe I finally got over Timmy. Maybe I just found what you said a little funny. Or it could be because you saved my life." He smiles.

"Finally a girl that laughs at my joke." I laugh at that and his smile widens. He starts to scratch his head.

"So do you think that the rest are done yet?"

"I would like to think so." We both smile as we walk out of the room. The whole group looks at us as we walk out of the room. Austin smiles.

"So I see that you two hit it off." I can't help but smile at that.

"Oh shut up Austin." He laughs and we start to walk.

We walk into the senior hall to see a group of more than twenty zombies. Felix motions for us to walk backwards. I hear the cock of a gun as we all start to walk backwards. Before we start to run, Felix says something but I don't understand it. I open the first door I reach; the rest follow me. I slam the door and I immediately regret doing it.

Right after the door slams, we all hear a symphony of moans closing in. Before they get here, I lock the door. I look at John and then at Felix, and John starts to talk.

"I think we should open the door to shoot them down, between Felix, hid dad and me we have enough firepower to at least kill all of them." Felix looks at him.

"He's right." We all look at Felix. I start to talk.

"I think that we need to open that door." He nods and the three people that are the best with guns move to the front of the group. I almost move to the back but Felix grabs my arm.

"I think you should open the door." I nod and move to the door and look back at the three people with guns.

"Are you ready?" Felix replies. "Yes."

I unlock the door and open it. I keep the door in front of me as a flood of zombies courses through the doorway. Gun shots go off and I grip the handle of the door until my knuckles go white. Minutes go by as bullets fly into the skull of undead monsters. Another few minutes go by and the bullets stop. I step from behind the door. I look at Everet and smile, and he smiles back. I step over bodies and I hear a moan from behind, but I don't have enough time to respond. Everet's smile drops and he screams.

A red hot searing pain ripples through my right arm. It starts from my shoulder. I pull my shoulder away from the zombie. I try to push it away, but my arm sears with pain when I try to lift it. I kick the zombie back. I can still see the chunks of my flesh in its teeth.

Everything slows down, and I scream. I look forward to see Everet running to me. My vision blurs, as tears run down my cheeks. It mixes with the blood on the ground. I fall to my knees as Everet bludgeons The zombie that bit me.

When the zombie falls down. Everet runs to me and I fall in his arms. I look up at him, as Felix rushes towards me. I can see tears in Everet's eyes. Felix's eyes start to water up. I start to talk.

"Why are you crying Everet? You haven't talked to me, before today." He smiles.

"I don't know why I am crying, maybe it is because one of my group members is dying." I smile as I look at Felix's hands, he is reloading his gun.

"Felix, I don't want you to shoot me." Felix starts to talk.

"I have to shoot you Alex." His voice is cracking.

"No, I want someone else to shoot me. I can't have you shoot me. I would rather Everet shoot me." He nods as Felix hands him over the gun.

"Everet, before you shoot me, tell me a pun." Everet, smiles as I look at him for the last time.

"You can't run through a camping site. You can only ran, because it is past tents." I smile, and laugh for the last time.

"Thank you for making me laugh. You know Everet, I finally figured out why you made me smile. I realized that I should have dated a guy like you. You wouldn't have left me. I want you to know that if I would have survived, I would have dated you." I see him smile, as I close my eyes. I hear a bang and I feel nothing.

CHAPTER 8

EVERET

After Alex's death we finished searching the school. After we get Martini and Malcobe from the houses we prepare a grave site for Alex.

Two days after we lower Alex in the ground I sit in front of Alex's grave, replaying the moment I pulled the trigger to kill a girl that was going to die. I hear the crunch of grass and I look behind me. I see Felix walking towards me.

"Why are you here Felix, don't you have to lead a group?"

"Everet, why are you crying over a girl you hardly knew?" My eyes sting from crying.

"I don't know why I am crying over a girl that I just met. Maybe it is just that she asked me to put a gun to her head and pull the trigger." I stop to take a breath and calm down.

"Why do you think that she asked me to pull that trigger? Out of all the people in that room, why did she choose me?" Felix's expression changes from a leader to a teenage boy who just watched his cousin died. He doesn't talk for what seems like a long time. He just stares at the wooden cross.

"I don't know why she asked you to do that. We will never know why she asked you to pull that trigger." He looks away from me, to look at the grave. Tears start to stream down my face as I sit in front of a grave for a sixteen year-old girl, who shouldn't have died.

"Felix, could you have pulled that trigger?" He doesn't even turn to answer me.

"No."

A week after my talk with Felix, I go to Alex's grave with Austin and Megan. Austin is the first one to talk after ten minutes of silence.

"So you've been for more than a minute and you haven't shed a tear. Have you gotten over it?" I stare at the cross and answer him.

"No. I don't know why but that scene of me pulling that trigger is the last thing I see before I go to sleep." I feel as if I just pulled the trigger again. I look at the two of them. Megan starts to talk.

"How did you get so attached to someone you only spent a few hours with?"

"I did not get attached with Alex." It is Austin's turn to talk to me.

"Why have you been coming out here every day for a week?" I look at him.

"You feel kind of guilty when you shoot someone and kill them." We all stop talking. I look over at Austin and Megan and they are hugging.

"You two can stay here but I am going to go back to the school." They answer in unison.

"We are going to stay here for a little bit more." Before I go I ask one more question.

"What was Alex like before the zombie apocalypse?" Austin looks back at me.

"She was strong and confident." I mutter one last thing before I go back to the school.

"She didn't deserve to die like the way she did."

CHAPTER 9

FELIX

"Trinity, what are we going to do?"

"What do you mean?" I look at her piercing green eyes.

"I don't know. I just don't know, I may act like I know what I am doing, but I don't. I mean I got my cousin killed." Trinity leans into kiss me but I move out of the way.

"Felix, you need to forgive yourself for that. It has been over two weeks. You can't say that you're the reason she is dead. She is dead because none of us saw the zombie behind her."

"Exactly, I didn't see it." Trinity stares at me and I decide to change the subject.

"So, do you want to go for a walk around the football and baseball field?" She smiles as she answers.

"Sure."

As we walk out of the building, I look over at Trinity.

"Why are you smiling?" Her smile makes me smile.

"Our first date was at a football game. Do you remember that Felix?" I start to smile.

"That date sucked."

"What do you mean it sucked? Oh I remember. You fell in a mud puddle." She laughs and I change the subject.

"So Trin, do you think anything will happen to us? I mean this is the zombie apocalypse and everything but do you think that everything between us will stay the same?" Her smiles slightly lessen.

"Yes, I am leaving you for John." I smile at that.

"No, but in reality, do you think that something may tear us apart? I don't think so, but do you?" We stop walking and she entwines her hand around mine.

"The only thing that I could see tearing our relationship apart would be if one of us die." I smile at that.

"I give you permission to date after I am gone." We start to kiss. I pull away from her.

"You know we aren't supposed to kiss on school property. Right?" She smiles.

"Shut up, Lee." Before we start to kiss again, I say another thing.

"Can you not use my middle name?" She just ignores me as I pull her closer. A loud scream takes us out of the moment. I pull away and look at her.

"We will continue this when I get back." I sprint back towards the school. When I get there I hear another scream. I enter from the back by the library. I hear another scream. I turn the corner and I run into John.

"John, what are you doing?"

"Looking for you. What are you doing?"

"Trying to figure out who I heard screaming." He stares at me and his face goes long.

"What happened?"

"We missed one and it got Everet's dad." I think about what he says for a moment.

"We missed a zombie? Ho…" I stare at John.

"Which room?"

"Follow me." I follow him through the halls. We hear another scream. John and I look at each other then we sprint. When we make it, I see Everet holding his dad in his arms and beside him is a dead zombie. The whole group looks at Everet and his dad. Everet looks up from his dad. His face is full of terror, as tears roll down his face. I whisper to John.

"Where is Emily?"

"She went to find Trinity." I nod and look back at Everet.

"What happened?" John answers for Everet.

"He went to look at the teacher's lounge and we missed that room, and the zombie bit him." I hear Everet whispering to his dad. He looks at me.

"Give me your gun." I take my gun out of the holster and hand it to him. I stare at him for a few seconds and wait for the bang of the gun. It feels like an eternity before the gun finally goes off, and when it does, I can see something changing inside of him.

. . .

I walk around the campus of the school with Trinity. I keep thinking about what happened to Alex and Michael.

"How did we forget about the teacher's lounge? I am the whole reason two people died." Trinity looks at me like I need help.

"It has been weeks since Michael died, you made a mistake. One mistake."

"I made two mistakes Trinity. One of the mistakes got Alex killed and the other got Michael killed."

"Felix, if you keep thinking that way you will blame yourself for everything. Felix, your actions saved people."

"They also killed people." Trinity stops walking and looks me in the eyes.

"You can't blame yourself for two deaths. If you do your actions will get more people killed. You have to forgive yourself." I stare at her for a long time.

"I know you're right but how do I deal with this. I have to hold back my emotions like a damn. If I cross my emotions with my actions, someone will get killed and I will be blamed for it." She is still staring into my eyes.

"You can damn up your feelings but just remember, it will come crumbling down. And when it does, I will be right by your side." I smile and she smiles. Trinity says one more thing before we change the subject.

"All we can do is hope that when the wall comes down, we will be safe."

"That's not the only thing we can do." She pulls me closer and we kiss. When I kiss Trinity, I feel like nothing can touch me. Like all the bad things in the world are gone. We both pull away, with a smile.

"What do we do now?" I smile at her.

"You know we have a couple of minutes before the sun goes down. I think we could kiss a little more." We smile at each other.

"Lee, the sun is going down. Let's just go check on Everet and then watch the sunset in the courtyard." I nod as I wrap her hand around mine. We walk to the football field talking about our past dates and what our favorite song is. Hers is Riptide by Vance Joy and mine is Living on a Prayer by Bon Jovi.

When we get to the football field, I see Everet sitting in front of the two crosses. We walk over to him, and start to talk to him.

"Hey Everet, we are going to the school." Everet stands up and looks at us.

"Sure." As we walk, Trinity and I are still holding hands. She starts to whisper in my ear.

"Do you think that we should be holding hands in front of Everet?" I don't answer.

"Don't you think that he is going through the same thing you are going?" This time I do answer.

"Yes, I know he is going through what I am going through, but way worse. You're probably right and that means we should un-hold hands." Our hands drop to our sides. I look over at her, to see that she is smiling.

"I don't think un-hold is a proper word."

"We have dozens of proper English grammar books at the school." I laugh at that.

"I like to read, but I will not read a boring English grammar book." Trinity just looks at me.

"You don't have to read the book." We walk closer to Everet.

"How are you doing Everet?" He looks at me with a blank expression.

"Fine."

"You're not fine."

"How do you know how I feel?" We stop walking.

"Everet, you just had to shoot two people who were on the brink of death. You're not fine."

"Felix, do not tell me about how I feel." Anger grows in his voice. "You don't know how I feel."

"Everet just calm down."

"I will not calm down." The anger is still in his voice.

"Felix, I don't blame you or anything. So just shut up and let me mourn." I nod and he starts walking to the school.

"Trinity, we better hurry."

"For what?"

"The sunset." She stares at me like I just ignored a friend dying.

"Are we just going to ignore what just happened?"

"Yes." She stares at me again.

"Why?"

"Because Everet ended the conversation." She drops it as we walk back to the school. When we get to the school, we go straight for the courtyard that has the best view of the sun setting. When we sit on the bench I wrap my arm around Trinity and pull her close.

"This is my favorite part of the day."

"Mine to." We sit there and kiss as the last specks of light finally give in and fade into darkness. We sit there for a while longer, and gaze up at the stars.

"You know my step-mom always told me that the best moments in life are when you are with the person you love." Trinity smiles as I talk.

"The best moments of my life have always been when you were around. I mean most of them are really stupid incidents, but they were also really funny." I kiss her one more time before we go inside. When we actually get inside, John and Emily are walking towards us. John has a smile on his face.

"What were you two doing out there?" I smile back at him.

"You know, just staring at the stars."

"I totally forgot that you were into that sappy stuff." He turns his gaze from me to Trinity.

"He watched the sunsets and looked at the stars even before you meet him." I smile at that.

"Let's go to sleep." They all nod as we start to walk to the rooms we have set up as sleeping quarters. The girls have one side of the hallway and the boys have the other. I smile at Trinity one last time, before she goes to her side.

. . .

"John, would you be able to kill Emily if she turns?" He stays silent for a few minutes.

"I don't know Felix, I don't know. Would you be able to kill Trinity?" I don't have to think about the question.

"No. I don't think I would be able to." We both look up at the sky and stay silent for a long time. I think about what would happen if Trinity died. I can't even imagine it. Then I think about Everet.

"John we need to talk to Everet."

"Why?" I keep staring up at the sky.

"He shot two people." He stays silent until we see Everet walking out of the school.

"Let's do this." He nods and we head for Everet. Before I start to talk to him, John gets on the other side of him.

"Everet we are here to talk to you." He looks back and forth between John and me.

"I don't need to be talked to." John pipes up.

"Yes you do."

"Explain to me how I need to be talked to." John looks from Everet to me.

"Well, you kind of shot my cousin and then your dad with the same gun and we see you come to their graves every day." Everet stops walking and looks both of us up and down.

"You think that I am depressed?"

"Yes. We do." He stares at me.

"Why can't you just leave me alone? I don't have depression. You would be the same way if you had to kill your dad and a girl you barely knew." John and I stay quiet as we watch Everet walk to the football field.

"He's right you know." I turn my gaze from Everet to John.

"Is he right or do you just hope he's right?" John stays quiet as he thinks.

"You're right."

. . .

"Felix, what do we say if someone wants to get in the school?" I look at Trinity as she stares up at the inky black sky.

"Depends on why they want to get in." She turns her gaze from me to the sky.

"What happens if the person wanting in is bad?" My expression goes cold.

"We will get to that when it comes." My gaze wanders from the sky to Trinity but is interrupted because she decides to get up.

"I am going inside." I nod.

"I am going to stay outside." She nods and we kiss. When I hear the shut of the door. A few minutes later, Austin and Everet walk out. Austin greets me first.

"What's up Felix?"

"Oh nothing, just sitting out here thinking." I look past Austin to see Everet staring at me like I tried to kill him.

"So Austin, why are you here?"

"Same here." Everet still looks at me.

"So, Everet why are you here?"

"I couldn't sleep." I nod and stare back at the stars.

I hear Everet and Austin talking but I don't pay attention. I just think. I get lost inside my mind thinking about what happened since the beginning of the zombie apocalypse.

CHAPTER 10

EVERET

I look in the mirror as tear fall into the sink. I keep thinking about how I shot two people. I stop sobbing as I walk out of the bathroom. I run into Felix as I walk down the hall.

"Were you just crying?" I don't acknowledge him as I walk down the hallway. I go into the nearest room and lock it. I sit in the nearest desk and let the tears fall. I stop crying when I hear a scream from outside of the window. I look out of the window to see a blonde girl fighting off a group of zombies. I run out the room and find Felix.

"I saw a girl on the road. She was fighting some zombies." He nods and I follow him out of the door.

"Shouldn't we go get some help from the rest of the group?"

"Everet, I think we can handle it. I mean there will be three of us and I think we can handle it." I look at him as we run to the gate. I can see the girl with her golden hair and dashing blue eyes.

When we get to the gate she turns from the zombies and looks to us. We open the gate, and she runs through it. One zombie gets through before we close it.

I kill the zombie while Felix closes the gate. After I kill the monster, I go to the girl.

"What's your name?" She stares at me like she can see what I've done.

"It's Charley." She smiles.

"I guess your name is Bob?" I smile for the first time in weeks.

"No, it's Everet and you're a really happy girl, seeing as how you just got almost eaten by five zombies." Felix walks over.

"You two can flirt. Just not right now."

"Felix, we weren't flirting. We were just talking." He smiles and whispers into my ear.

"You were flirting with her and she was flirting with you." I walk away from him to talk to Charley again.

"This is the place where we live." She nods.

"Is the guy who is with you the leader person or something?" I think that for a little bit.

"Kind of." She nods.

"So, do you want to go meet the rest of the group?"

"Yeah." I nod and look at Felix.

"Felix, let's show…"

"Stop right there Everet. I think you should show Charley around the school." I whisper to him.

"Thank you." He nods, and walks away.

"So, Charley I am going to show you around the school." She smiles and nods as we walk.

"So this is the beginning of the school." She stops me before, I can continue.

"I don't need the tour. I went to this school." I nod.

"How old are you?"

"Fifteen."

"Cool." We stay silent for a little while. Before, we go back into the school, she stops me.

"Can you show me where you stay?" I nod, and we walk into the school.

"So Charley, what happened to you since the beginning of the zombie apocalypse?" She tenses up.

"I was visiting my grandpa when everything went down. We stayed there for about a week, then we went to my house. My grandpa went first." There is a break in her voice.

"Look, if you don't want to talk about it, then you don't have to." She nods.

"Just let me finish please." I nod and listen to her.

"It was only my dad and me. We were still at my house. Within the first couple of weeks, we ran out of food. My dad went out to go find some but he never came back." Her voice breaks even more.

"My aunt lived in the house across the street from the school. She is the only family I have left. So I decided to try to find her." My face goes long.

"Your aunt wasn't there."

"What do you mean?"

"We stayed at the house across the street the night before we came to the school, we found nothing there. No one was there, we also didn't find any blood." She nods and we continue walking.

"At least she isn't dead."

"Yeah." We keep walking and we almost run into Austin. He looks shocked. He takes me aside.

"Why are you talking to a girl that I have never seen before?"

"She was at the gate and she was in trouble so Felix and I let her in."

"Oh. Ok." I nod.

"I was just taking her to the rest of the group." He nods and he starts to walk with us.

"Her name is Charley." Austin nods.

"So Charley did you come to this school before the outbreak?" She nods yes.

"Cool." We stay silent for the rest of the walk. When we get to the hall where we sleep, I call the rest of the group. They all come out to see why I called them. Malcobe looks like she already knows her.

"This is Charlie, she was fending off five zombies when Felix and I found her. Megan can you show her where to sleep?" Megan nods and I turn to Charley.

"If you need me, I will most likely be at the football field or walking around the school. Ok?" She nods and I walk away with Austin following. As we walk away, I hear the group talking to Charley. Before we go down the hall, I look back to see Charlie looking back at me, before she disappears from my view. Austin flashes his usual grin.

"So, are you going to make your move?" I look at him like he said the dumbest question in the world.

"What, I am not going to make a move on her. She probably isn't even interested in me."

"Well, seeing as you just met her she isn't interested in you. That only changes when we talk to someone. All you did was…"

"I don't need relationship advice from you." He nods and we continue to walk. Instead of going to football field or walking around the school, we go to the library.

"You know Austin, ever since we got here. The library has got to be one of my favorite places in the school."

"I never knew you liked to read."

"Well I do, and ever since we got here I have read. It helps me take my mind off of things." He nods and starts to walk around.

"You know, in Texas, the library was my favorite place in the school. The librarian was one of my favorite teachers." I nod, while looking for another book to read.

"What was her name?"

"Mrs. Newman. She was the head of the library club, which was my favorite club I joined. The best part about the library club was setting up and helping during the book fair." I nod.

"I stashed a flashlight in the librarian's desk in the upper right drawer. Can you get it for me?" I hear him walk over to the desk and open the drawer.

“Here catch.” I turn around from the books on the wall to Austin. He throws the flashlight and I catch it. I turn on the light and the beam shoots and splatters all over the books.

“You know Austin, I know you must of have watched a lot of zombie movies and read a lot of zombie stuff, but all those things never actually prepare you for the actual thing. It is just a glimpse into the world of death and decay.”

“Yeah. Truth be told, I never actually thought I would make it this far. I thought that I would make it a month.” I look at all the books, and I hear footsteps down the hall. I look at Austin and Charley enters through the door.

“Hey Charley.”

“Hey Everet.” She smiles.

“So do you like reading?”

“There really isn’t anything else to do.” She nods.

“I always liked reading.” I nod and glance over at Austin and he is leaving the room.

“So Charley, what kind of music did you listen to?”

“I really don’t listen to music.”

“Cool.” I nod.

“You really didn’t talk to a lot of girls did you?” I smile at her.

“You know, I did.” She nods as she walks around the room.

“Want to go walk around the hall. Now that the halls are dark, it looks like a horror movie.” She smiles and I stand up.

“You know some people would call walking around the dark hallways more of a love moment than a horror moment.” She smiles at that.

“Well, I would tell those people that the characters have to progress, rather than just scary action all the time.” We smile at each other.

“So I see you liked to watch horror movies.” Charley smiles.

“I was a movie buff.” I nod as we walk out of the room.

"Is that flashlight in your pocket or are you just excited to walk with me?" My face goes red.

"It is totally a mini flashlight." She laughs.

"I could have told you that it was mini." I laugh with her.

"You know if you get too scared…" I stop. I think back to what happened to Alex.

"On second thought Charley, I need to go and do something." I walk down the hallway and I run into Austin.

"So what happened with Charley?" I walk pass him.

"I have something to do." I don't stop walking till I get out of the building. Austin comes right after me.

"What happened back there?"

"I don't know. Before, Alex got bit, she smiled at me like Charley just did."

"Look what happened to Alex was not your fault. It was a freak accident, we missed one." Charley walks out.

"Hey Everet, what happened back there? One minute we were having a nice time and the next you zoned out, and walked away."

"I don't know." She nods and drops the subject. "I am just going to go back to the room where the girls go." I nod and watch her go back inside.

"I'm going back to the library." Austin nods and I walk back into the school. When I get to the library I see Charley looking at the walls of books.

"Charley I thought you said you were going back to the hallway where we set up."

"I changed my mind half way down the hallway." I nod and walk to one of the computers.

"Wanna go and smash one of the computers?" She smiles.

"Sure." I pick up the monitor at the librarian's desk.

"Do you want to carry the big thing under the computer?"

"You mean the CPU?"

"You were a big tech nerd, huh?"

"No, that's just common knowledge." I nod.

"Do you want to carry it or not?" She nods, and we walk out of the room.

"So Everet where are we going to destroy these?" I smile.

"I kind of want to throw it over the fence at the concrete." She smiles.

"Cool." We laugh as we walk out of the building. As we walk to the front of the fence we hear moans and the smell of rotten flesh is strong. Before we get past the gym I see a group of about ten zombies at the gate about to open the gate. Charley and I squat down.

"Charley, if one of them move their arms up by the little flimsy handle of the gate, there will be chaos." She nods.

"We need to back up and go back in the school, before the gate gives up." I look back at the gate and more zombies are gathering at the gate.

"Ok, when I start moving, you move." She nods. I start to move, but the handle of the gate moves up and the monsters start to flood through the gate. I start to move and I don't hear Charley behind me.

"Charley, we have to move." She just stands there. I look at the group of zombies shuffling towards us.

"Charley we need to move now." She doesn't reply. Instead of trying to talk to her again, I grab her arm and move to the gym. I look back at the monsters; they are getting closer. I open the door and I pull Charley in the gym. With the power out, the gym looks like an inky blob. I reach into my pocket and pull out the tiny flashlight.

I turn it on, and I look at Charley.

"What happened back there?" She snaps out of it and looks at me.

"I… I don't know. That's how my Grandpa died in a big group like that." I nod.

"Why'd you leave me in the middle of the hallway?"

"I don't know."

"Don't give me that bs. I know something happened. You still haven't recovered from it; I can see it in your eyes."

"What do you mean you see it in my eyes?"

"Well, first off, you said that I could find you at the football field and I asked Megan what that's about and she told me what happened." I look shocked.

"What did she tell you?"

"She told me about Alex and your dad and you act like I don't know what it means to lose someone."

"Charley, can we please talk about this later." She nods.

"There is a way to get out in the locker rooms."

"What do you mean?"

"Well when they built the building, they put a door in the locker rooms to get out in case of a fire." I nod and point the light to the boy's bathroom.

"We are not going through the boy's bathroom." I stare at her.

"Well, we are not going through the girl's bathroom."

"Haven't you wondered what a girl's bathroom looks like?" Before I can answer we hear a moan and the smell hits me now.

"You didn't check the gym did you?"

"Apparently not." Charley lowers her voice.

"Why didn't your group check the gym?"

"We will talk about this later. We have no time and you have no weapon."

"Neither do you." I look at my belt where I usually keep my hammer and it is not there.

"Ok Everet on the stage is a door that leads to a room with all the things that we used in P.E. and during P.E. we played softball."

"So you're saying that we make our way from one end of the gym to the other, in pure darkness, not knowing where the zombies are."

"That's exactly what I'm saying."

"Let's do this." I point the flashlight from the bathroom to the stage. I hear more moaning. I look at Charley.

"On three we run." She nods and we get ready to run.

"One." I look over at Charley and see how she is anticipating the start.

"Two." I hear more moans.

"Three." We sprint towards the stage. The light shakes and I see the glimpse of an arm. I look to the side at Charley to she is behind me. I make it to the stage first. I point the flashlight behind me to see Charley jump on the stage.

"I didn't see anything during the run. Did you?"

"I saw an arm." She nods.

"Show me where the bats are." She nods and walks over to a door that seems rickety. The door is already open when we get there. Charley takes the light out of my hand and walks in the little room and comes out with two softball bats and hands me one.

"Charley, we are going through the boy's room." She nods and we walk off the stage and down into the boy's locker room. There is a small window that shines a little bit of light. I shine my light around and I see a shirtless zombie with a bite on its hip. It must have been changing into his P.E. clothes when it died.

"I'll take this." Charley nods as I hand the small light to Charley. I walk to the zombie and I grip the bat with both hands and I swing. The bat connects and shatters the skull. Blood splashes over me and the lockers. I look back at Charley, and I hear another moan.

"Let's get out of here before something happens." I nod as I look for a door. I see one and I head for it. Charley is right behind me. When I open the door the fresh air burns the rancid air out of my lungs.

"We didn't die. You didn't die. I didn't die." I smile at Charley, and she smiles back. I hug her.

"We should probably let someone know about the gym." I laugh at that.

"Let's go see if the group killed the zombies." She nods as we walk to the courtyard. The group of zombies is by the door where we walked out of the school.

"Well, we're screwed." Charley looks at me.

"Not with that attitude." I smile at that.

"Wanna just go to the front?"

"Sure." We walk to the front of the school and we go through the front doors.

"Let's go tell the rest of the group. She nods and we run to the rest of the group. We run into Austin.

"Where is Felix?" He looks at me.

"What happened?"

"There is a group of zombies at the entrance to the freshman hall and we need to clear out the gym." He stares at me.

"I thought we cleared out the gym."

"That's what got you. Not the thing about the group of zombies at the hallway." I sigh.

"Austin, tell the rest of the group to get their weapons. I am going to find Felix." He nods and runs down the hall. I look at Charley.

"Are you with me?"

"Everet, I just blindly ran through a gym with you. I am still with you." I nod.

"I think that Felix is in the courtyard."

"If Felix is in the courtyard, he should have seen the zombies." I nod.

"Then he is probably walking around the football field." She nods.

"Follow me." I nod and she runs to the fire exit door and I follow her. We run through the door and we hear a gunshot and we look at each other.

"Do you think that Felix heard that?"

"Obviously." I nod and we run back through the door, and to the freshmen hall. We see John and Felix running to the library. They look at us, and motion us to go with them. We run after them. When we get to the library I start to talk.

"Felix, we need to clear the gym when we get the chance." Felix nods as he says the next thing.

"When were you gonna tell me that there was a horde of zombies coming to the entrance to the school?" I start to lie.

"I'm sorry, I froze when I saw the horde coming through the gate. Charley took me to the gym to escape them." He nods. A banging on the door keeps Felix from answering. We all look at the door. Charley starts to talk.

"So, why did you let them in?" Felix and John just look at Charley.

"Well, we opened the door, because we thought that there were about five out there. Instead of ten." Charley and I nod. Charley looks at John.

"John, did I have you in my chemistry class?" John answers her question.

"Yeah, we were partners in dissecting the frog." She nods.

"So what are we going to do? We heard one shot and seeing as both of you have guns." Felix listens to me and thinks.

"John stand about ten feet back from the door. Everet and Charley get to the back of the room. I am going to open the door." We nod.

"I really don't think this will work." Felix nods and starts to rub his thigh.

"Why don't you think it'll work?"

"Don't you remember what happened to Alex?" He sighs.

"That will never happen again."

"How do you know Felix? How do you know?" He keeps rubbing his thigh.

"We can't do this right now." I nod.

"Let's do this then." He nods and Charley and I walk to the back of the room.

"Everet, if this is the end, I don't want to die without kissing a guy." I blush.

"You've never kissed a guy." She nods and Felix opens the door and the first gunshot goes off. We look at Felix and John shooting into the ocean of zombies. After a few more minutes of shooting, they finish. I smile as I look at Charlie.

"Well, we didn't die." She smiles.

"Yeah." She blushes.

"Why are you blushing?" Before she answers, Felix walks up to me and whispers into my ear.

"Kiss da girl. La la la kiss da girl."

"Really a Disney movie reference."

"Yep." He walks away and I look back at Charley.

"He wants me to kiss you." She nods and I blush.

"Have you ever kissed a girl?" I nod my head.

"It was at a playground when I was six" She smiles.

"That doesn't count." She stares at me.

"This does." I look into her eyes and she pulls me close to her. She puts her lips on mine. I feel shocked for a moment, then I close my eyes and kiss back. After a few seconds she pulls away.

"I am going to see if everyone is alright." She runs out of the library. I look at John and Felix.

"Well. That happened." Felix just laughs.

"Yeah."

"Can you tell me what actually happened?" He smiles.

"Well you just had your first kiss and she ran away."

"Cool." I feel stunned.

"Should I go after her or something?" John answers this one.

"Just let her calm down."

"I didn't get into a fight with her, I kissed her." Felix smiles.

"Just remember that was her first kiss too." I nod as I stare at the doorway.

"I really don't know what to do." John looks at me.

"I am telling you to just let her cool down." I nod and walk to the door and walk over dead bodies. Felix asks me something as I walk down the hallway.

"What are you going to do?"

"I'm going to close the gate."

CHAPTER 9 FELIX

I slide down the railing of the stairs as Everet walks up to me.

"Everet, did you chain the fence?"

"Yeah I did that weeks ago." I nod.

"Did you ever talk to Charley?"

"Yeah." I nod.

"How is our food supply?"

"That is why I came to talk to you."

"You're saying that we need to go on a run?"

"Yeah." I start to rub my thigh.

"Ok, get my dad and John. Plus, you're coming with us." He nods.

"We leave in an hour. We go down the road. We can't go up the road yet." He nods.

. . .

"Dad isn't there a grocery store down the road?"

"I think there is a Fred's down there. We can stop there. All we have to do is just hot wire a car." I nod.

"Charley, after we get out of the gate, chain it." She nods. We walk out of the gate and I hear the clink of the gate, as Charley closes the gate. We walk down the highway looking for a car to high jack. Less than twenty minutes out my dad finds one.

"Ok, this car should do. I mean it has enough seats and it has enough space for our cargo." The door is still open. My dad pulls a knife from a sheathe on his belt. He walks to the opened door. Nothing is in the car.

"Come on, get in the car." We nod as we get in the car. My dad hot wires the car and we start to move.

"So dad how much longer till we get to the store?"

"About twenty minutes." I nod as I look out of the window. All I see are houses that are probably abandoned. I look from the window to John.

"How many people do you think are left?"

"In the state?"

"No, I mean in the country."

"Oh, I would have to say about at least over one hundred thousand."

"What makes you say that John?"

"Most people don't know how to handle this." I look at him.

"Most people can't handle seeing the people they love being killed." I nod and I look back out of the window. Twenty minutes later I see the store and I see someone walking out of it.

"Dad, that's the…" We hear a bang and a thud then my dad loses control of the car, and we skid and hit a pole in the parking lot. I hit the seat in front of me, and I feel a blinding pain and my door flies open. A muzzle of a gun is pointed at my head.

The man pulls me out of the car and I fall on the ground and the blinding pain is worse. The gun is pointed at me again. This time is see the face behind the gun. I almost bite my tongue

"You're one of the guys from the highway."

"Shut up." He pulls me to my feet and starts to bark an order.

"Walk." I start to walk and I see John, Everet and my dad with a gun to their head. They make us walk into the store and they put us in chairs, then they tie our hands. A familiar voice erupts through the store.

"You know when you're abandoning your car, it's always wise to take the map." My dad answers.

"You know that stealing is illegal." A thug smacks my dad. The man pulls out a gun and shoots my dad in the thigh. My dad screams. I wince at the sound of the last of my family screaming.

"Can you tell me your name? You know if I am gonna die, I kind of want to know my murder's name." He cracks a smile.

"My name is Matt."

"How can a big scary ma…" I get hit. Blood trickles down my chin. John smiles.

"You know that was a smack of a time." He gets hit. Matt gets irritated.

"I really hate kids that disrespect their elders. You should also know I know where your people set up." His smile grows larger.

"I also know that two of your people have died." He looks at all of us, and I try to hide the fear. I say something to hide the fear.

"Well looks like we have a little stalker on our hands." Matt's smile fades a little.

"You are a little ignorant bastard you know that right?"

"I also have a high pain tolerance." Pain flares through my body as he smacks me.

"You're going to need it."

CHAPTER 10 FELIX

"John, I have started to hate this place." He nods.

"Felix, I want you to know if we die, you were the greatest friend I have ever had" I smile, this seems like it will work.

"Thanks John. I feel the same about you." Everet pipes in.

"What about me?"

"You were an amazing friend." He smiles.

"You were to." Matt walks up from behind.

"You know, you have all been good guests but we have to cut your time short." The anger grows.

"This isn't one of your crappy puns is it?" He laughs.

"God you are a smart ass."

"I know, I've been told that." Matt smiles.

"We are going to the school…" My dad launces at Matt, but before my dad can do anything, Matt shoots him right through the heart.

"Now is probably a good time to tell you that won't be the first death caused by me." My tears fall to the floor. The anger floods through me like blood.

"You bastard." He smiles.

"I know, I've been called that." Before, he walks away I say one thing.

"I will kill you."

"I hope you do."

All that drives me at this point is anger. We just need to get out of this hell hole. So I start to improvise

"Dude can you take these plastic zip ties off of me."

"Shut up." I nod.

"Please." He just says shut up again.

"Ok, I'm going to take that as a no."

"Can you at least give me a more comfortable chair?" John smirks.

I wink at Everet, and he winks back.

"Hey thug guy. Can you come see, I kind of have to go use the bathroom?" He walks to Everet, and I stand up with the chair. I turn around, and I push the chair into the thug's back. He falls, and I kick him in the head.

"You know guys, I forgot one small part of the plan that is going to de rail this whole plan." John sighs.

"You forgot you were tied to a chair, and you realized that you have no way to cut the zip tie." I smile.

"You realized that from the start didn't you?"

"Yep" I look at Everet and John.

"Anyone have a bright idea?" Everet pipes up.

"Try banging the chair against the floor like in the movies." I try that, and I realize that the movies were wrong. So wrong. Painfully wrong. The chair is still on my back, and I look at Everet and John. I see fear on their faces.

"Is this a cliché movie moment, when the villain is behind me?" They nod, and I look behind me. The cold steel is pressed against my forehead.

"Just get on with it." He hits me, and I fall on my side. The chair strapped to my back makes it worse. I drop into unconsciousness, the moment I hit the ground.

I wake up in a moving vehicle and everything hits me. I see John sitting next to me.

"Did I really pass out on the floor of a store?"

"Yes." Everet is sitting on the other side of me.

"Felix, I think he intends to kill one of the people at the school."

"We can't do anything right now." They nod, and I realize that there might not be any way out of this.

"Look till we get to the school, we need to be quiet." They nod, as I start to make a plan to avoid dying in an hour.

. . .

When we get to the school Matt's men push us out of the car, and forces us to open the chain. I look at Everet.

"Do you still have the key?"

"Yes." He opens the gate and we walk through. Matt starts to instruct us.

"We are going to walk to the front door, and into the hallway, where your group set up camp. I look at John and Everet.

John, Everet, and I lead Matt and his men to the hallway where the group is. When we get to the hallway, I yell for the group. They all walk out into the hallway, instantly fear soaks through the room the worst part of it is Malcobe has Elliot in her arms.

"Guys we have a little problem." I look around the room to see fear creep into everyone's faces.

"This is Matt, and we kind of shot him on the road a few months back, and when we went to get food, he shot out our tire. Then he killed my dad." My voice weakens when I say the last part.

"Then we attacked on of his guards, which made him mad. I think he is still mad." The fear grows stronger with every second that they stand there looking at me.

I look over at Trinity. Rage and fear mixes inside me. Matt sees me looking at her, and whispers into my ear.

"She dies first."

"You're an ignorant whore." He punches me in the gut.

"Why can't you make this easy and be a good little boy?" I bend over and smirk through the pain.

"I don't know why I can't be a good little boy; all I know is that your mom is a giant whore." He pushes me to the ground and kicks me.

"You know I am getting tired of you." Before, he can say another thing I say something.

"That's what your mom…" He kicks me again, then picks me up by the collar of my shirt and I feel the cold steel being pressed against my head.

"How are you surviving being beaten down by a grown adult?"

"Maybe I'm just a tough son of a bitch." He smiles.

"You know you remind me of you me. A smart ass, and a dumbass." Anger courses through my veins.

"You know Matt I don't like you, I just think that you're an ass, who killed my dad. Plus, I am nothing like you." His smile dampens.

"You're a brave little boy."

"That's what your mom said." He hits me on the back of the head with the butt of the pistol, and I drop to the floor. My vision goes blurry, and I try to get back up, but he kicks me back down. I look up at the group.

They try to act like they are tough, but its fading. I stare at Trinity. Remembering how I felt when I first kissed. Remembering how I love her. Remembering that night when we sat and watched the stars. My vision fades, and the last things I hear is a gunshot and a baby crying.

Stay tuned for the next novel by

Michael McClendon

to be released late 2016!

For updates on the author, to schedule him for a literary event or to find out about his latest projects visit

www.MMcClendon.com

www.ingramcontent.com/pod-product-compliance
Ingram Content Group UK Ltd.
Pitfield, Milton Keynes, MK11 3LW, UK
UKHW041939190726
13854UKWH00004B/1676